MEET THE GIRL TALK CHARACTERS

Sabrina Wells is petite, with curly auburn hair, sparkling hazel eyes, and a bubbly personality. Sabrina loves magazines, shopping, sleepovers, and most of all, she loves talking to her best friends.

Katie Campbell is a straight-A student and super athlete. With her blond hair, blue eyes, and matching clothes, she's everyone's idea of little miss perfect. But Katie has a few surprises for everyone, including herself!

Randy Zak has just moved to Acorn Falls from New York City, and is she ever cool! With her radical spiked haircut and her hip New York clothes, Randy teaches everyone just how much fun it is to be different.

Allison Cloud is a Native American Indian. Allison's super smart and really beautiful. But she has one major problem: She's thirteen years old, five foot seven, and still growing!

Here's what they're talking about in
Girl Talk

RANDY: I can't believe Stacy spent all of
          the money for the seventh-grade
          Earth Alert Fair!

ALLISON: I know, and the worst part about
          it is that she spent the money on
          amusement park rides that pollute
          the air — those rides are totally
          against the theme of the fair.

RANDY: I still say we should tell Mr.
          Hanson about this. She had no
          right to use the money without
          asking us first.

ALLISON: Well, that's Stacy. We'd just better
          come up with a way to save the
          fair — and fast!

EARTH ALERT!

By L. E. Blair

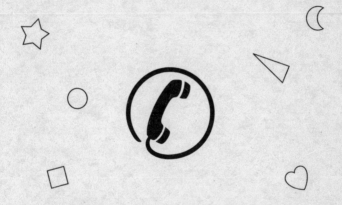

GIRL TALK® series created by Western Publishing Company, Inc.

Produced by Angel Entertainment, Inc.

Western Publishing Company, Inc., Racine, Wisconsin 53404

Text by Lea Jerome

Chapter One

"Your name's Allison, right?" a boy's voice asked from somewhere behind me. It was Monday morning, and I was standing in front of my locker at Bradley Junior High, where I'm in the seventh grade.

I turned around to see who was talking. A boy I'd never seen before was standing there smiling at me — his teeth were very white in his tanned face. His straight hair was very, very light blond and reached almost down to his shoulders. Peeking out from beneath his bangs were eyes such a light shade of blue that I had the feeling I could almost see right through them. I noticed that he was wearing about ten of those woven friendship bracelets on his left arm. He also had on a tie-dyed shirt, loose-fitting white pants, and sandals with thick, rainbow-colored socks.

"Allison Cloud," I replied softly, looking down at him. Even though I'm only thirteen,

I'm 5'7," so I find myself looking down at almost everyone at Bradley. Anyway, it was pretty unusual to see someone that tanned in Acorn Falls, Minnesota, especially when it wasn't even hot out.

"Hey, Allison," he said. "I'm Arizonna. Love that name, Cloud. It's really cool. What is it?"

"It's a Chippewa name," I told him.

"Chippewa?" He flashed me another grin. "As in Native American?"

I nodded. I've never lived anywhere but here in Acorn Falls, but both my parents were born on a reservation. My grandparents lived on one for a long time before they came to live with us.

"Very cool," the boy said again. "I knew there was something special about you."

For a moment I just looked away. It felt kind of weird to have a complete stranger say something like that to me.

"So you're Arizonna?" I asked, trying to change the subject. I remembered how he had introduced himself.

"Yeah," the boy replied. His pale blue eyes crinkled up at the corners as his smile widened.

"You know, like the state, but with two n's."

"Oh," I murmured, not knowing what else to say.

"Listen, Allison," Arizonna continued. "I heard about your idea for the Seventh Grade Fair. The environment is like *the* issue of the 90's, and I think an Earth Alert Fair is very."

"Very what?" I asked. I was starting to get the impression that Arizonna and I were speaking two different languages.

"Just, you know — very," Arizonna replied. He shook his long blond bangs out of his eyes. The way he was looking at me was making me feel kind of like an amoeba on a slide under a microscope.

"I know it's only my first day here at good old Bradley Junior High, but I really want to help you organize the Earth Alert Fair," he continued, before I could even think to ask him.

"You do?" I asked in surprise. Every year the seventh graders sponsor a fair and donate the money to a local charity. I had suggested using an environmental awareness theme for this year. I thought we could use the proceeds to set up recycling bins at Bradley for paper, aluminum cans, and glass bottles.

Last week we held a class vote and most of the seventh graders liked the idea of an Earth Alert Fair. They also voted me in charge of the fair. My first act as Earth Alert Fair chairman was to announce a special meeting at Fitzie's for this afternoon. So far, no one had mentioned showing up at the meeting — except for my three best friends, Sabrina Wells, Randy Zak, and Katie Campbell. And now, Arizonna.

"Like, definitely," he replied, nodding.

I smiled. "Great. We're getting together at Fitzie's today after school for our first meeting."

"Fitzie's?"

"It's a restaurant and ice cream place," I explained. "A lot of kids from Bradley go there after school."

"So, right after school at Fitzie's," Arizonna said. Just then the warning bell for third period rang. "I'd better go. Where's this Fitzie's joint, anyway?"

"Two blocks away, on the corner of Main and Sycamore," I said, pointing in the general direction.

With a quick nod and a grin, Arizonna turned and ran off down the hall. "Catch ya' later, Allison Cloud," he yelled over his shoulder right before he rounded the corner.

I stood there a moment longer, staring after him. I was glad Arizonna was going to help with the Earth Alert Fair, but I wasn't at all sure what to make of him. I had never met anyone quite like him before.

Shaking my head, I grabbed my English books from the top shelf, shut my locker, and hurried to class. I got there just as the bell rang, so I quickly walked to my seat behind Katie. The pink barrette holding back Katie's straight blond hair was right in front of me, and I noticed that the color matched her pink-and-white-striped sweater dress. Katie's very neat and organized. I guess we're a little alike that way.

Katie, Randy, Sabs, and I all have third-period English class together, which is our homeroom, too. I didn't have a chance to say a word to my friends, though, because at that moment the loudspeaker crackled and hissed, and Mr. Hansen, our principal, began the morning announcements.

After the announcements, Ms. Staats, our English and homeroom teacher, gave us a pop quiz, and we spent the rest of the class going over it. I love English, so the quiz was pretty easy. In fact, I actually enjoyed it.

When the bell rang, Ms. Staats called me over to her desk to talk about a district-wide essay contest. She told me that she thinks I have a very special talent for writing and that I should enter. Hearing that from my favorite teacher made me feel pretty good, especially since I think I would like to be a writer some-day. The essay deadline wasn't for a few months, but I immediately thought of doing something about the environment and the Earth Alert Fair.

I mulled over the idea as I walked to the cafeteria for lunch. None of my friends had arrived yet so I picked out an empty table and opened a book while I waited for them. Reading is one of my favorite things to do.

"Allison, did you see that new guy?" Sabs asked breathlessly, moments later, as she threw herself into the chair across from me. "He's gorgeous!"

The thing I love most about Sabs is that she's always bursting with energy. She's very petite, and everything about her is bouncy and bubbly. She even bounces when she's sitting still! Right now, her curly auburn hair was bobbing around her face, and the fruit on her tray was rolling around.

"You mean Arizonna?" I asked her, closing my book and taking out my lunch. I should have known that Sabs would have already met him. She loves to meet new people. It's not as if I hate it, but I'm not really comfortable around people I don't know. At least, not at first.

"You know him?" Sabs asked, her hazel eyes opening wide. "His locker's near Katie's and mine, so we met him this morning."

Shaking my head, I told her, "No, I don't know him, but he volunteered to work on the Earth Alert Fair." I brushed my long black braid over my shoulder, then took a bite of my chicken sandwich.

"Seriously?" Sabs exclaimed. "That's really cool. Did you know he's from L.A.?"

I hadn't known, but that explained why Arizonna talked the way he did. I had seen TV shows where people from Los Angeles said things like "radical" all the time.

"Hey," Sabs continued, sounding really excited, "do you think Arizonna knows any famous people? Maybe he knows some directors or producers or something. Maybe he could introduce me to some. This could be my big break! Oh, my gosh, I could just die!"

Sabs wants to be an actress when she grows up. If you ask me, I'd say she's one already. She was in Bradley Junior High's production of *Grease*, and she totally stole the show as one of the characters, Frenchie.

"Just because Arizonna's from Los Angeles doesn't mean he knows those people," Katie pointed out. She had come up while Sabs was talking, and put her tray of lasagna on the table. "I bet lots of people from California don't know any celebrities at all."

Katie is very logical, while Sabs, on the other hand, gets so excited about everything that she tries to say a million things at once and doesn't always think things through. I think they balance each other out really well, but sometimes it's funny to hear the two of them having a conversation.

"Well, you never know," Sabs said, not at all discouraged.

"Where's Randy?" I asked, looking around the cafeteria and not seeing her anywhere.

But I did see Billy Dixon. I smiled in spite of myself when I saw his thick, dark curly hair and the leather bomber jacket he always wears. I'm usually shy around boys, but Billy and I got to be friends a while back when I tutored him in some of his classes. I think he's really a special person.

Billy used to have a reputation as a troublemaker, and when I first met him he was really moody and angry. But then we found out that part of the reason he had problems in school was that he had a reading disability. Now that he's getting help for it, he has a much easier time with his schoolwork. Right now, he was talking to someone in the intense, moody way he has. Suddenly, he looked up and caught me staring at him. Billy waved at me, smiling, and I waved back.

"Hey, Al, are you going to eat all of those cookies?" Sabs asked.

I turned back to my friends and pushed the bag of homemade peanut butter cookies toward her. "Here, have some. Nooma always packs extra for everybody." Nooma is the Chippewa name I call my grandmother.

"Like me, for instance," Billy said, appearing at our table. He sat down next to me and reached over to take two cookies. "Hi, everyone," he said. "Where's Randy?"

"Right behind you," Randy said, pulling out the chair next to Billy's and sitting down. She pulled her black bowler hat down on her head so that just the ends of her black spiky hair stuck out from beneath the brim. Besides the hat, she was wearing a floral-print cotton dress that looked like something out of the 1940's, and white socks rolled down to the tops of her clunky black shoes.

Randy is without a doubt the most outrageous of my friends. She moved here from New York City at the beginning of the year, and she lives in this big converted barn with her mother, whom Randy calls M. Randy likes to wear really crazy outfits. I love them, but I could never dress like her. I suppose I'm just more quiet and conservative.

"How's project Earth Alert going?" she asked me, taking a carton of yogurt from her lunch bag and popping the lid off.

"I think it's great that everyone liked your idea, Al," Sabs piped up. "I mean, it's a chance to do something really important."

Katie nodded. "It's kind of exciting to think that we can really make a difference in helping to save the environment."

"So, do we have any new volunteers yet?" Randy asked. "Or is it still just us? I can't understand how everyone likes the Earth Alert thing but no one wants to help."

I shrugged. "We just voted on the idea yesterday," I pointed out.

"I could help," Billy offered, looking at me.

I turned around to look at Billy. It made me really happy that he wanted to be a part of the fair. I hadn't been sure he would want to, since, like me, he doesn't always feel comfortable with group activities at school. Smiling at him, I said, "That would be great."

"Arizonna wants to help, too," Sabs put in, grabbing another peanut butter cookie.

"Arizona?" Randy asked. She raised an eyebrow at Sabs, looking at her as if she were crazy. "The state of Arizona wants to help out at our Earth Alert Fair?"

Sabs laughed. "No, Arizonna the new student," she said.

"Like the state, but with two n's," I added, remembering Arizonna's comment.

11

Turning to me, Billy asked, "Is that the guy with the long blond hair?"

"He's so incredibly cute," Sabs said in this rushed, excited way she has of talking. I could tell she had a crush on Arizonna. "Don't you think so, Al?"

"I guess so," I replied. I suppose he's cute in his own way. I can understand why Sabs thinks he's good-looking, anyway.

"He told me that in his old school, they surf during gym," Sabs continued.

Randy looked up from her yogurt. "That sounds kind of cool. Surfing's a lot like skateboarding, you know." Randy skateboards everywhere whenever there's no snow — which isn't very often around here during the winter.

"So, that's why you were late for homeroom, right, Al?" Sabs asked suddenly, snapping her fingers. "You were talking to Arizonna, weren't you?"

I nodded.

"He's going to help with Earth Alert?" Billy asked. "When's the first meeting?" I noticed that he was looking at me with a weird, kind of intense expression, and his gray-blue eyes were blazing.

Before I could ask Billy what was going on, Sabs told him, "Today, after school, at Fitzie's. Hey, I bet I could talk Sam, Nick, and Jason into it, too." Sam is Sabs's twin brother, and Nick Robbins and Jason McKee are Sam's best friends.

"Good idea," Katie agreed. "We can use all the help we can get."

I could feel that Billy was still looking at me, and when I turned to him, that moody, unreadable expression was still in his eyes.

"I'll definitely be there," he said. Standing up abruptly, he muttered, "I've got to go."

"Hey, you didn't finish your cookies —" I said, turning back to him, but he had already walked away, his hands shoved into his jeans pockets.

As I finished my lunch I wasn't sure what to make of Billy's behavior. The way he had just acted reminded me of how he used to be when I first met him — kind of like he was ready to fight the whole world. I could tell something was bothering him, but I didn't know what.

"Hey, Al," said Katie, drawing my attention back to the table, "I think maybe Billy's feeling a little jealous."

I stared blankly at her. "What are you talking about?" I asked. "Jealous of what?"

"Arizonna," Randy answered.

"What?" I asked automatically. "Why would Billy be jealous of someone we've all just met?"

Sabs looked kind of surprised, too. But then she twisted an auburn curl thoughtfully around her fingers and said, "It could be true, you know. I mean, you did agree with me that Arizonna's cute."

"But I didn't mean it that way," I protested. I couldn't believe Billy would misunderstand me like that, but my friends all seemed to agree that that was exactly what had just happened.

Boys are so hard to figure out.

Chapter Two

"I can't believe it!" an angry voice exclaimed later that afternoon, while Randy and I were changing into our gym clothes in the girls' locker room. "An Earth Alert Fair! How bogus!"

Randy looked at me and rolled her eyes. The voice was coming from the next row of lockers, but we didn't need to see the girl to know that it was Stacy Hansen. She's the principal's daughter, and she's kind of stuck-up and phony.

I decided to ignore her comment. Pulling my sneakers out of my gym locker, I sat on the bench behind me and put them on.

"I think your idea was much better," said another voice that I recognized as Eva Malone's. Eva is Stacy's best friend. "The Romance Fair would have been great!"

"Definitely," Stacy agreed in a smug voice. "I mean, just think— tunnel of love and a kiss-

15

ing booth would have been perfect."

"Who'd want to kiss a fish face like her's?" Randy whispered to me, sucking in her cheeks and making a face like a blowfish. I put my hand over my mouth and stifled a giggle.

Needless to say, Randy and Stacy do not get along. In fact, none of us are friends with Stacy.

"Earth Alert!" Stacy practically spat out. "Who even cares?"

"Arizonna does," Randy called out.

I was starting to feel as if we were eavesdropping, so I was glad Randy had spoken up.

"I wouldn't believe anything Randy Zak says," Eva said loudly. "She's just trying to bother us, Stacy."

"He's even helping to organize it," Randy added, grinning at me.

I'm pretty shy about standing up to people, especially bossy people like Stacy. But nobody can get Stacy's goat like Randy can. She knew as well as I did that if a new cute boy was involved in our Earth Alert Fair, that would make Stacy really jealous.

"Do you think Arizonna's really going to help them?" Stacy whispered to Eva. She obviously thought we couldn't hear her. "I mean, he's so incredibly cool."

"He's a major hunk!" Eva whispered back, "I'm sure Randy just made that up. Don't worry about it, Stacy."

"But what if she's telling the truth?" Stacy asked, still talking in a hushed tone. "I don't want him to think I'm not into the environment."

I knew it wasn't any of my business, but it bothered me that Stacy would pretend to be interested in the environment just to get the attention of a cute boy. It made me feel awful to think that she would abuse a good cause that way. Suddenly, I didn't want to hear another word she had to say about it.

"Come on, Al, lets go," said Randy, shutting her gym locker. I think she understood what I was feeling. Randy's like that. She comes off really brash, but underneath she's a very sensitive person. She grinned, waggling her eyebrows up and down in a really comical way, and I could tell she was trying to cheer me up. "It's time for my all-time favorite and yours — Dodge Ball! I'm sure the skills we learn from playing this game will help us later in life. Aren't you?"

I couldn't help laughing. Gym isn't my favorite class, but it did feel pretty good to do something physical. It completely took my mind off what I had heard Stacy say in the locker room.

That was our last-period class, so as soon as gym was over we rushed to get changed, then hurried up to our lockers. I didn't want to be late getting to Fitzie's. After all, I was in charge of the fair.

We made it there in less than ten minutes, and I was relieved to see that no one else had arrived yet. Randy and I staked out a big booth in the back and ordered sodas. I pulled out my notebook and uncapped a pen, then looked around Fitzie's. The place was already starting to get crowded.

"Hi, guys," Katie said a moment later, sliding into the booth next to Randy and shrugging off her hockey team jacket. "I'm not late, am I?" Katie is on the boys' hockey team, which I think is really admirable.

Billy was right behind her. "Do you want some of my sundae?" he asked, putting his banana split in front of me and handing me a spoon as he sat down next to me. "So, what are we doing for this fair?"

"That's what this meeting is about, you bozo," Randy said, bopping him playfully on the head with her bowler hat. "I'm sure Al's got some ideas, though, right?"

I nodded, glancing at the list I'd already written out in my notebook. I hoped everyone would like my suggestions.

Ten minutes later, Sabs flew into Fitzie's and threw herself down next to Billy. "Hi, you guys," she said breathlessly. "Sorry I'm late. I had a little problem with my locker."

"What's wrong with our locker?" Katie asked. She and Sabs are locker mates. "It was all right when I left it."

Sabs launched into a long story about the door being stuck open and her having to find a custodian to fix it. I don't know why, but that sort of thing happens to Sabs all the time.

Sabs was still talking when I heard a voice call out, "Allison Cloud!"

I looked up and saw Arizonna standing just inside the entrance to Fitzie's, looking around. "Are you in here, babe?" he called.

"Babe?" Randy echoed, looking at me with a grin. "I presume that's Arizonna."

I nodded, feeling my face turn bright red. I didn't think anyone had ever called me babe before in my entire life.

"We're back here!" Sabs yelled, standing up and waving.

It was easy to follow Arizonna's progress as he made his way through the crowd to our booth. He had on a bright orange nylon bomber jacket. It was the kind of nylon they make parachutes out of. His tie-dyed shirt peeked out from underneath his jacket and he looked like a walking rainbow.

"Allison Cloud," he said looking right at me, as he stopped in front of the booth. "So this is Fitzie's. I guess it's kind of very, in a Minnesota sort of way."

Katie giggled. "Very?" she mouthed at me.

"Hi, Arizonna!" Sabs exclaimed.

"What's up, Sabs?" he asked, flipping his blond bangs out of his eyes. "Hi, Katie." Then, looking at Randy and Billy, he flashed an easy smile and added, "How y'all doing? I'm Arizonna."

Randy introduced herself, but Billy just glared at Arizonna. Billy leaned back in the booth and slung his arm loosely around my shoulders. I was surprised Billy did that. It felt strange but at the same time I liked it.

"Uh, and this is Billy Dixon," I told Arizonna, feeling a little uncomfortable that Billy wasn't acting very welcoming. I noticed that Arizonna looked from me to Billy and back to me again.

"How do you like it at Bradley so far?" Sabs asked excitedly. I don't think she even realized she was breaking the tension, but I was relieved that she did.

"Cool, but I miss the waves," Arizonna answered. Then he sat down next to Katie. "Well, I'm ready to go," he continued, looking at me.

"We're waiting for my brother," Sabs said, wrinkling her nose. "He said he had to pick something up in the gym before coming here. Of course, he's late."

Just then, I heard Sam's voice from somewhere in the crowd. "Nick, I told you we didn't have any time to shoot hoops. Now I'm never going to hear the end of it from Sabs."

"Why?" Nick asked as he, Sam, and Jason stepped out of the crowd in front of our table. "Oh, they're all here already. Oops."

"Hi ya, Nick," Billy said, laughing and giving Nick a high five.

I remember when Sam, Nick, and Jason didn't like Billy at all. I guess they thought he was kind of tough, and he thought they were goody-two-shoes. But ever since Billy and I have been friends, they've all gotten to know each other a lot better. Sometimes they even hang out together.

"B.D.!" Sam exclaimed. "What's going on?"

"Don't act like you're not late," Sabs announced, crossing her arms over her chest. "I told you not to be late."

Randy and I exchanged a look and grinned at each other. Of course, Sabs would never admit to Sam that she had been late herself. Ever since she and Sam ran for seventh-grade class president and vice president, Sabs has made it her personal project to turn Sam into a "human being," as she says. Even though they won the election, Sabs says she still has a long way to go with his rehabilitation.

They bicker all the time, but you can tell that they are really close. I guess it's because they're twins. They've done all these studies on the special bond between twins. Looking at Sabs and Sam, I definitely believe it.

"Arizonna," Arizonna introduced himself, with a nod to Sam, Nick, and Jason. He pulled a neon green baseball cap out of his back pocket and put it on, flipping the brim up.

"What?" Sam asked, sounding confused. "What about Arizona?"

"That's his name, Sam," Sabs said, sounding exasperated. "Like the state, but with two n's."

"Oh," Sam replied blankly.

"I'm Nick, that's Sam, and this is Jason," Nick said, squeezing into the booth next to Sabs while Sam and Jason pulled up some chairs. It was getting kind of crowded, but I was happy to see so many people wanting to help out with the Earth Alert Fair.

"Let's start," Randy announced, as soon as the boys had figured out what they were going to eat. "Take it, Al."

"Well . . ." I began slowly. I was finding it a little hard to think, with Arizonna staring at me so intently. "I thought we could play some games."

"What do you mean?" Sam asked, sounding confused. "Volleyball or something? Nothing personal, Al, but that sounds kind of lame. Maybe we can come up with something better."

Arizonna emptied half of the orange juice he had ordered, in one long gulp. "Maybe that's not what she means," he said to the other guys, then turned his pale blue eyes to me. "What kind of games, Allison Cloud?"

"The games I'm thinking of were created hundreds of years ago by Native Americans." Since Native Americans lived harmoniously with nature, I thought the games would be appropriate for the Earth Alert Fair. "They're played using only things that are a natural part of the Earth."

Thinking about the games made me think of my grandparents. I know some kids might not like having their grandparents live with them, but I really love having mine around. They've taught me and my little brother Charlie a lot of Chippewa customs. Knowing the old traditions makes me feel proud of my heritage.

"Excellente!" Arizonna exclaimed enthusiastically. "Like, what kind of games?"

Feeling encouraged, I continued, "Well, one of them is a game called Hacky Sack. Lots of people still play it now. I bet you guys know the game: it's when everyone passes around a small round leather sack using only their feet, trying not to let it hit the ground."

"I've played that game," Nick said, sitting up straight. "It's the best."

"Yeah, I've played it, too. I never knew it was a Native American game, though," Katie commented.

I nodded, and took a bite of Billy's sundae. It was delicious. "Originally, the game was only played by women," I explained.

"Seriously?" Randy asked. "That's wild."

"That sounds really rad," Arizonna said. "You know, Hacky Sack is huge in L.A. — especially on the beach."

Next to me, I heard Billy mutter, "That's just great," under his breath.

"So, what kind of food are we going to have?" Sam spoke up, licking his lips. "Hot dogs and stuff?"

"What about, like, natural foods?" Arizonna suggested. I looked up at him, startled. I had been about to suggest the same thing.

"You mean, like, sprouts and stuff?" Nick asked, grimacing. "I'd rather have a hot dog."

"I think natural food is a good idea," Randy put in, looking forcefully at Nick from beneath the brim of her hat.

"Yeah, a hot dog kind of goes against the whole Earth Alert thing," Sabs added. "We don't want to serve any meat or anything packed with preservatives."

"Why don't you handle the food?" I asked Randy, writing it down in my notebook when she nodded. "Oh — Randy," I continued, suddenly remembering another thought I had had. "Do you think Iron Wombat would like to play at Earth Alert?"

"Cool!" Randy exclaimed. "Definitely."

Brushing his blond bangs out of his eyes, Arizonna looked at Randy and asked, "What's an Iron Wombat?"

"That's my band," Randy told him. She pulled her drumsticks out of the pocket of her jacket and beat out a quick drumroll on the table. Randy never goes anywhere without them. She says that she never knows when the impulse to play will hit her.

"Jamming!" Arizonna exclaimed.

Randy tapped my notebook with a drumstick, saying, "I think we should play using only instruments that don't need an amplifier."

I could tell by the gleam in her black eyes that she was really excited about the idea. "You know, just acoustic guitars, not electric, and a piano instead of an electric keyboard."

"What a great idea," said Katie, crunching down on the ice cubes from her soda. "That way you won't use any electricity at all."

"I play acoustic guitar," Arizonna put in. "And I'm, like, really into writing my own stuff. Do you mind if I jam with you, too?"

"That would be cool," Randy told him. "I'll check with the other guys in the band."

"So, Allison Cloud," Arizonna went on, changing the subject. "What else do you want us all to do?"

I wished he would stop using my last name all the time. It was making me feel a little self-conscious. I could tell it bothered Billy, too. His arm was still draped over my shoulder, and it kept tensing whenever Arizonna said anything to me.

"Well, uh, what does everyone want to do?" I asked quietly. I thought that would be the best way to start organizing.

"I'll help Randy with the food," Katie said, and I wrote her name next to Randy's in my notebook.

"We'll need posters and stuff, right?" Sabs

asked. "I'll do that."

"Me too," Nick added.

When I finished writing their names down, I looked up to find Arizonna staring at me.

"What are you going to do, Allison Cloud?" he asked.

I stared down at my list for a moment. "I guess I'll work on the games," I replied, seeing that no one had volunteered for that yet.

"Like, I'd be into that," Arizonna said. "Count me in."

I noticed that Sabs seemed a little disappointed that Arizonna wasn't going to be on the poster committee. To tell the truth, it made me feel a little uncomfortable to know I'd be working with Arizonna. I guess I was just really aware of how tense Billy was acting around him. And I didn't want to hurt Billy's feelings or Sabs's.

"I'll work on the games, too," Billy added in this determined voice. Then, looking at me, he said, "Listen, I've got to go."

Nick and Sabs stood up to let him out of the booth, and without saying another word, Billy was gone. "I've got to get going, too," I said. "I promised my mother I'd be home in time to help with dinner. We're having company tonight." It was true, but I also wanted to be alone to think about what was going on with Billy and Arizonna.

Closing my notebook, I stood up. "I'll see you guys in school tomorrow. Randy, we have to meet with Mr. Hansen about the food budget at sixth-period study hall, okay?"

Randy sighed. "My favorite person," she said. "No problemo."

I waved at everyone and pushed my way out of Fitzie's. I was really surprised when Arizonna fell into step next to me a moment later.

"Allison Cloud, I'll walk you home," he said.

"That's okay, Arizonna," I protested. "You don't need to."

But Arizonna didn't pause. "So, this is Minnesota," he said.

Seeing that he wasn't going to leave, I decided I might as well be nice to him. "Is Acorn Falls very different from L.A.?" I asked.

"Very," Arizonna replied, nodding so that his bangs fell over his eyes. "It's almost always hot in L.A. and there's a ton more people. You know, dudes everywhere! And the smog is so thick, I think this is the first time I've seen the sun clearly since I was two years old."

I giggled. "Why did you move here?"

"My parents got divorced," Arizonna stated matter-of-factly. "My dad and I moved here, and the mother unit and my three sisters are still in L.A. I would have stayed with my mom, but my parents, like, felt this was a good time for me to have a male role model."

I didn't know what to say, so I just nodded. Luckily, Arizonna just kept talking. He told me all about his old neighborhood and how close the beach was to his house. I could tell he really missed the ocean.

It's funny, I could walk for a half hour with Billy and not say two words, and neither of us would try to fill the silence. But Arizonna didn't let the conversation lag for a second. I didn't think that was bad, just very different. When I got to the corner of Spencer Avenue, where I live, I paused to say good-bye to Arizonna.

"Allison Cloud, since you're my first buddy in Acorn Falls, I want to give you one of these," he said, untying one of his friendship bracelets. He took my left arm and tied the bracelet onto my wrist. "Now, we're official friends."

"Thank you," I said quietly. I thought that was really sweet of him.

"I have a feeling we'll be friends forever, Allison Cloud," he continued. Then he turned and headed back down the sidewalk the way we had come. "I'll catch ya'."

"Good-bye," I called after him.

I fingered the bracelet, which was bright yellow with red and orange stripes. It was really beautiful.

It's just a friendship bracelet, I told myself. It really doesn't mean anything special.

Chapter Three

"How much money do we have left?" I asked, shifting uncomfortably in my chair. Randy and I were sitting in Mr. Hansen's office on Tuesday afternoon, and the news the principal was giving us was anything but good.

"Two hundred dollars," Mr. Hansen replied, leafing through some papers on his desk. "As I mentioned, most of the budget went to renting the rides. Last night, Stacy told me it was all arranged. She made the phone calls from my office this morning."

"We never knew anything about it," Randy told him through clenched teeth. I could tell she was really mad, and so was I.

We had just found out that Stacy had spent most of the fair budget on rides — a roller coaster, Ferris wheel, and motorized stuff like that. It was bad enough that she didn't say anything to me about it, but all of the rides used gas and polluted the environment.

Stacy had actually told her father that she was the co-chairperson of the seventh-grade fair, even though she had made it very clear to me and my friends that she didn't want any part of Earth Alert Fair. I guess she'd changed her mind after learning that Arizonna really was helping us out with the fair. I knew I couldn't tell our principal that his own daughter had lied. So now we had no choice but to accept Stacy as my co-chairperson for real.

To make things worse, the money we made on the fair was supposed to go to an environmental cause. Now we'd probably have to use the money to pay for the rides. And we still had to buy food for people who came to the fair! To be honest, I had no idea what we were going to do.

"Well, I'm sorry if there's been some misunderstanding, but I'm afraid it's too late to do anything about it," Mr. Hansen said, looking from Randy to me. He pushed the papers on his desk back into a manila folder. "The deposits are nonrefundable, and I dropped them off at lunch myself."

"But — " Randy began in a very angry tone.

"That's okay, Mr. Hansen," I said, cutting her off and standing up. "We'll figure something out."

After he handed me an envelope with the remaining money, I thanked him, and Randy and I walked out of the office.

"I can't believe Stacy!" Randy exclaimed, as soon as we were out in the hall. "I can't believe that she would pull something like this!" Her dark eyes were flashing angrily. "What nerve!"

I didn't say anything. I just stood there and let Randy vent her frustration. Randy's the kind of person who gets mad quickly, but once she lets it out, her anger blows over.

"I think we should have told him she was totally lying about being co-chairperson," Randy went on.

"What would have been the point?" I asked, shifting my schoolbooks to my other arm. "You heard Mr. Hansen. The deposits are nonrefundable. We can't get the money back, anyway."

After a slight pause, Randy sighed and said, "And it's not like we can tell Mr. Hansen that Stacy lied about being co-chairperson. I guess you're right, Al. Like it or not, we're stuck with these rides, and with Stacy the Great."

Smiling wearily at Randy, I asked her, "What do you think we should do about the food now?"

"I guess The Good Earth is out," she said.

Randy had given me the price list of a natural foods caterer she knew about, and I pulled it from my notebook. "We couldn't even feed a quarter of the kids with the money we've got left," I said. "We'd better think of something else."

"And soon," Randy added. "Earth Alert's a week from this Saturday. That's less than two weeks away. Katie and I will get going on this problem right away."

Just then the bell rang, and the hallway immediately began to fill up with kids rushing to their next classes. "I think everyone on the planning committee should meet this afternoon to figure out what to do," I said, raising my voice above the noise. "This is an emergency."

"Definitely," Randy agreed.

We found Sabs at her locker, and she offered to hold the meeting at her house after school. Still, by the time I got out of my last class and went to my locker to get my jacket, I was feeling discouraged about the fair. I wasn't sure how we were going to solve our food problem, and I was a little worried about what else Stacy might pull behind our backs.

"Allison Cloud!" Arizonna suddenly exclaimed, appearing at my locker. "I've been, like, looking for you forever, babe. Where have you been hiding?"

The look on his face was so cheerful, I couldn't help smiling back. Then I spotted Billy at the end of the hall. He, Sam, and Nick were walking right toward Arizonna and me. Somehow, the situation made me nervous. My palms even started sweating a little.

"Hi, Al," Sam said, as they got closer. "How are ya', Arizonna?" He slapped Arizonna on the shoulder. "I heard about what happened in English. That was cool. Mr. Stover deserved it. He's a terrible teacher."

Arizonna nodded. "Thanks, dude."

"What happened?" I asked them.

"It was great," said Nick. "We were reading a poem by Walt Whitman, and Stover was talking about Whitman's life and how to interpret the poem and all. That's when Arizonna told him off."

"You did?" I asked, surprised. I was very

glad I had Ms. Staats as my English teacher. I had heard that Mr. Stover wasn't very good — that he taught right out of a textbook and didn't listen to anybody else's opinion. I would hate an English class like that.

"What did you say?" I asked Arizonna.

"I said that poetry was real personal, and that, like, there was more than one way to read it. That dude thinks his opinion about what the poem means is the only right one! Unbelievable!" Arizonna replied.

"You really did that?" I asked Arizonna. I thought it was great, the way he'd stood up to Mr. Stover.

Nick let out a whistle, saying, "Man, you should have seen Stover's face! He sent Arizonna to Hansen's office so fast!"

I looked back at Arizonna. "Did you get in trouble?"

"Nah," Arizonna said. "The principal dude just gave me a warning — something about my being new in school or whatever, and not knowing how you dudes do things."

"I don't believe it!" Billy muttered, sounding angry. "If I pulled something like that in Stover's class, I'd probably get suspended!"

I turned toward Billy, startled. I had been so caught up listening to Arizonna's story that I didn't see Billy join us. He looked really mad, but he was probably right about getting suspended. Some teachers thought of Billy as a troublemaker, even when he wasn't doing anything wrong. That wasn't fair, but Billy was acting as if it was Arizonna's fault that Mr. Hansen hadn't given him detention. I didn't think that was fair, either.

"Uh . . . listen, Al," Sam said, shooting Billy a glance and changing the subject. "I heard about the money problem. Are you coming over to my house now?"

I nodded, but my eyes were still on Billy. He wasn't looking at me, though. In fact, he was acting as if I weren't even there.

"There's a problemo?" Arizonna asked. He didn't seem to be bothered by Billy's comment at all.

"Stacy rented a Ferris wheel and roller coaster and now there's almost no money left in the budget," Jason explained. "I mean, a roller coaster sounds fun, but there's got to be food, too."

A frown crinkled Arizonna's tanned forehead. "A roller coaster's going to pollute the air," he pointed out immediately. "I'm sure it uses gas."

"I never thought of that," Sam admitted after a pause.

"That's exactly why we're having an Earth Alert Fair," I told him. "To make people think."

Sam nodded. He looked a little worried as he glanced at his watch. "We'd better get going," he said to Nick and Jason. "Sabs will kill me if we're late again."

I was about to ask Billy if he wanted to walk me to the meeting, but he suddenly said, "I've got to go." Spinning around, he walked away.

"Check ya' later, B.D.," Sam called after him.

Looking after him, I suddenly realized that I had been talking to Arizonna and not saying a word to Billy. Even though I felt hurt at the way he was ignoring me, I wondered if he thought that I was ignoring him. I decided I'd better talk to him and find out what was really bothering him.

Telling the other guys I'd meet them at the Wellses', I ran after Billy.

Billy didn't slow his pace at all. I didn't

catch up to him until he was almost at the front door of the school.

"Where are you going?" I asked breathlessly, touching him on the shoulder. He paused at the door but didn't turn around. "I've got stuff to do," he replied gruffly. "More important than this fair, that's for sure."

"I thought you wanted to help out," I protested. I tried not to show how hurt I was that he would talk that way about the Earth Alert Fair when he knew how important it was to me.

"I changed my mind," Billy said. He finally turned to look at me, and I saw that his eyes were like distant blue-gray clouds. "What's it to you anyway, Allison?"

"What do you mean?" I asked.

He gave a short, sarcastic laugh. "Looks like you've got all the help you need, Allison," he answered, glaring at me.

For a second I just looked at Billy. I couldn't believe he was acting this way. "Billy, if something's bothering you, I wish you would just talk to me about it. I don't think you understand —"

"Don't worry about it, Allison," Billy interrupted, then I saw he was staring at the friend-ship bracelet Arizonna had tied around my left wrist the day before.

"Billy — " I began to explain, but when I looked up. Billy had already gone through the door. He was walking very slowly with his hands in his pockets. I opened the door and called after him, but he wouldn't look back. A moment later, he was gone.

Chapter Four

My fight with Billy seemed to set the tone for the whole week. Nothing went well.

The only thing we agreed upon at the emergency meeting at Sabs's house was that we had better include Stacy in our planning. Not everyone was crazy about that idea, especially since that probably meant Stacy's friends — Eva Malone, B. Z. Lattimer, and Laurel Spencer — would want to help, too. But when I pointed out that it would be better to include them than to have Stacy plan the rest of the Earth Alert Fair behind our backs, everyone agreed.

The problem was, every time I tried to corner Stacy and set up meetings, she made excuses not to talk to me. By Friday afternoon, I still hadn't been able to pin her down, and I was feeling very frustrated about it. The fair was only a week from tomorrow, and we still had to plan everything.

Finally, we had no choice but to make the arrangements without Stacy, and we planned a big meeting for Saturday at Sabs's house. I knew we'd get everything done, but I wasn't happy about doing it all at the last minute.

Friday after school, I called Billy's house and left a message about Saturday's meeting. I had been hoping he would change his mind and decide to be a part of the Earth Alert Fair. I hadn't seen him since the beginning of the week, and every time I'd called his house, his brother told me Billy wasn't there. I wasn't sure if I should believe him or not.

Billy was definitely avoiding me, and that hurt my feelings. It made me feel a little angry, too. I knew Billy was upset about Arizonna, and I also knew that if he would just talk to me about it, he would see that there was nothing to be upset about. It wasn't my fault he wouldn't even speak to me. But that didn't make me feel any better.

I was happy when it was time for Saturday's meeting. At least working on the fair would take my mind off Billy.

"Al! It's terrible!" Sabs exclaimed when I arrived at her house Saturday afternoon. She pulled me inside and back to the Wellses' kitchen, where Randy and Katie were sitting at the kitchen table, eating some chocolate chip cookies.

"What is it?" I asked. The worried way my friends were looking at me made me kind of nervous. "What's wrong? Where's everyone else?"

"At Eva Malone's house," Randy told me.

I looked at her, feeling puzzled. "Eva's? But the meeting's supposed to be here." I sat down, resting my notebook and pen on the table.

"Stacy the Great did it again," Katie explained, reaching for a cookie. "She arranged a different meeting at Eva's house."

"And didn't even tell us about it," Sabs finished dramatically. "If we don't get over there fast, who knows what they'll do!" Tugging her New York Yankees baseball cap over her forehead, Randy said, "Hey, don't worry. They're probably busy planning fun, environmentally safe entertainment. You know, like setting off a nuclear bomb or something."

I laughed in spite of myself. "How did you find out about the meeting?"

"Arizonna told Sabs," said Katie. "And

44

Stacy told him and everyone else. Except us, that is."

"Maybe we shouldn't even go. You know, as a kind of protest," Sabs suggested. "Except that Arizonna will be there. I mean, he is cute and all, but if you think we shouldn't go . . ."

"I think we have to go," I said, looking at my friends. "I don't like the fact that Stacy is trying to elbow us out of the way, but there isn't time to have a war with her about it. I think we have to work with her as best as we can."

Sabs, Katie, and Randy looked at each other, then nodded.

"Righto, as usual. It's a good thing one of us has her wits about her," said Randy, getting up from the table. "Okay, let's roll."

Ten minutes later, we were standing on the sidewalk across the street from Eva's house.

"I can't believe we're about to walk into Eva Malone's house," Randy said as she stared at the split-level brick house. "Willingly."

Sabs giggled. "I think it's kind of funny. I mean, we're the last people she would want to come over."

Randy flipped her skateboard up with one

foot and caught it in her hand. "As Arizonna says, it will probably be very."

We all laughed, but I was feeling a little preoccupied. I really wanted to get this meeting going. "Don't you think we should go in?" I asked. "That's the only way we'll ever get the fair planned."

Nodding, Randy linked arms with me and Sabs, who grabbed Katie. We all crossed the street together like that, marching up the Malones' front steps and ringing the bell. I was very surprised when Arizonna answered.

"Allison Cloud!" he said happily when he spotted me. "What's up, dudettes?" he asked everyone else. "Come on in. We're all in the back room."

"Hi, Arizonna," Sabs greeted him, stepping in first. From the way Sabs was blushing, I could tell she still had a crush on Arizonna. "Is my brother here?"

Arizonna nodded. "Sam was the first one here — after me, that is. Said something about being worried you would get here before him. That dude lives in fear of you."

"Good," Sabs said, and then giggled. "I guess his training is beginning to take."

"Hey, you guys!" Nick called out as we stepped inside Eva's family room. Nick and Stacy and Eva were sitting on a brown and green couch against the wall. Sam was in an upholstered chair, his legs swinging over one arm, while Jason, B. Z. Lattimer, and Laurel Spencer were sitting cross-legged on the carpeting, with a big bowl of popcorn between them.

I noticed that everyone said hello, except for two people — Stacy and Eva. They definitely looked surprised to see us. I had a feeling they weren't going to make this meeting easy, so I decided to get down to business right away.

"So, what have you guys talked about so far?," I asked, looking right at Stacy as my friends and I took seats around the Malones' family room.

"We were just, like, starting," said Arizonna, throwing himself on the floor and stretching out, his hands behind his neck. "So, babes and dudes, what do you want to do first?"

"Let's start by going over the committees we've already organized," I began before Stacy could open her mouth. I had decided that the Earth Alert Fair was too important to let Stacy take over, especially since she didn't even seem to care about the environment. That meant that I would have to take control of this meeting myself. Since I'm usually pretty shy, it felt kind of funny, but also good.

I quickly read over the list of people who had already volunteered to work on the food, posters, music, and games.

"I can help with the posters," B.Z. offered, which made me happy. Maybe there was a way for all of us to work well together after all.

"Don't forget to mention the rides," Stacy said in a snotty voice, reaching for a handful of popcorn. "We can't overlook the main attraction, you know."

"Stacy might be right," Nick put in.

Randy looked at Nick as if she couldn't believe she'd heard right. "You can't be serious," she said. "Those rides pollute the air."

Swinging his legs to the floor, Sam said, "I think Nick's right. I mean, a lot of kids might show up just to ride the roller coaster, and stuff like that. Once they're there, it's our job to educate them about saving the environment."

"I suppose so," I answered slowly, biting my lip. "But it doesn't send out a very good message about saving the environment."

"Oh, come off your high horse, Allison," Stacy said, making a kind of snorting noise. "Who cares? As long as it's fun."

Arizonna pushed himself up to a sitting position and looked at Stacy. "I think you're, like, missing the point, babe," he told her. "How can we expect people to believe we're really serious about saving the planet if we're, like, not setting a primo example ourselves?" He glanced back over his shoulder. "Right, Allison Cloud?"

I nodded. Stacy was glaring at me, but at least she didn't say anything else about her rides. In the end, we decided that the rides should be set up in a totally separate part of the school from the rest of the fair. I thought the Earth Alert message might come through more strongly that way.

I don't know how I managed to do it, but by the time our meeting was over, we had gone over every single thing on my list. Sabs's poster committee would do the posters tomorrow and hang them up on Monday. Laurel sounded pretty interested in the Native American games, and she offered to help organize that part of the fair with Arizonna and me.

Randy said that everyone in Iron Wombat was "totally psyched" to play for the Earth Alert Fair, and that the band was even writing a new song with a special Earth Alert theme. She said the other guys in the band thought it would be great to have Arizonna play with them, and that she was going to try to get some other bands, too.

Randy also came up with the idea of doing a mural for the fair. She suggested painting a slice of life in the rain forest. It would show all the birds and plants and everything, and then a bulldozer on the very edge of it. I thought that would be perfect. Sabs and I volunteered to help her paint it on huge poster paper in the gym. When it dried, we would hang it on the wall by the soccer field, where the fair was being held.

Jason and the other guys offered to help Katie and Randy price different kinds of natural foods. I thought that was pretty nice, considering they don't even like health foods.

Stacy, of course, kept trying to boss everyone around. After what Arizonna had said about her rides polluting, she decided she wanted to be in charge of selling tickets.

"I think we should sell them ahead of time. Advance sales are very important." She shot a look at Eva, who of course nodded her agreement.

I just looked at Stacy. "But the seventh-grade fair tickets have always been sold the day of the fair," I told her.

"Yeah," Katie added. "Why make extra work for ourselves ahead of time? We already have tons to do."

The rest of the kids agreed with us. In the end, Stacy and Eva didn't volunteer for a single committee except for the rides.

"So, Arizonna," Stacy said in this sugary voice when the meeting was pretty much over, "how do you like Acorn Falls so far?"

I really didn't feel like sitting around while Stacy tried to flirt. Since we had made just about all the arrangements, I decided to leave.

"Um, I have to go, everyone," I said, getting to my feet.

"Sounds good to me," said Randy as she, Katie, and Sabs joined me.

Saying good-bye, we left the family room and walked down the hall to the Malones' front door.

"Allison Cloud!" Arizonna called as Randy opened the door. I turned to see him walking down the hallway toward us. "Hang out a sec!"

When he got to us, he looked uncertainly at Randy, Sabs, and Katie. I had the feeling he wanted to talk to me alone, and that made me very uncomfortable.

"Uh, we'll wait outside," Randy said, sizing up the situation. She pushed Katie and Sabs out the door, then closed it behind them.

"Allison Cloud," Arizonna said again. "I'm sorry about all these rides and stuff. But I guess we're, like, stuck with them."

I nodded, peering curiously at him and wondering why he hadn't just said that in front of my friends. I had the feeling that I was looking into the ocean, his eyes were such a clear, light blue.

Then Arizonna reached over and lightly touched the friendship bracelet on my wrist. "Do you, like, want to take in a flick with me after the fair on Saturday?" he asked.

"Um . . ." I began. I was totally taken by surprise. I didn't know what to say, and the intent way Arizonna was staring at me made it hard for me to think. "I guess so," I finally managed to blurt out.

"Cool!" he exclaimed. "I'll call ya'." With a wave and a grin, he turned and went back down the hall.

I felt completely dazed as I opened the door and rejoined Randy, Katie, and Sabs. They all looked at me with these excited, expectant expressions on their faces.

"What did he want?" Sabs asked.

"He asked me out on a date," I said slowly.

"What!" Randy, Katie, and Sabs exclaimed all at the same time.

Sabs's face kind of fell, and that made me realize what I had just done. I had agreed to go on a date with a boy one of my best friends had a crush on!

"For next Saturday. And I said yes," I added miserably.

Stepping past my friends, I started walking slowly down Eva's front walk. It was amazing how I woke up so happy today and how now I felt worse than I've felt in a long time.

Chapter Five

"Allison, what's the matter?" Sabs asked, catching up to me. She had a kind of worried look on her face. "You don't exactly sound excited about going out with Arizonna."

Before I could say anything, she blurted out, "I mean, I hope it's not because of me or anything. I think it's great that he asked you out."

"But I don't really want to go out with him, Sabs," I told her.

Sabs looked relieved to hear that, but now Katie was looking at me strangely.

"So why did you say you would?" Katie asked, putting her hands in her jacket pockets.

I took a deep breath, trying to figure it all out. "I guess I just didn't want to hurt his feelings."

"Well, if you don't want to go on the date, then you shouldn't," Randy said decisively.

Somehow the problem didn't seem that simple, though. "I already said yes," I protested,

54

"so I think I'm going to have to go. I really don't know how to tell him no after I just agreed to go on the date."

"That's really tough," Sabs said sympathetically. "Let me go through my magazines tonight, and see if I can find any articles that tell you how to handle something like that."

"Thanks," I replied. Sabs subscribes to tons of magazines, but I didn't think any article was going to help me. "You know, I think Arizonna's really nice and I'm glad we're friends, but — "

"Ohmygosh!" Sabs suddenly exclaimed, cutting me off. "What about Billy?"

I hadn't even considered that. But now that Sabs had brought it up, I started to feel even worse about the date with Arizonna.

"That's right," said Katie. "He's already mad at you. Didn't you say you were pretty sure he backed out of the fair because he thinks you like Arizonna?"

I nodded. Billy was definitely not going to understand about this date.

"There's only thing for you to do, Al," Randy said, turning toward me.

"I know, I know," I said, guessing what she meant and dreading having to do it. "I'm going to have to go tell Billy myself."

Sabs's hazel eyes opened wide. "Seriously?"

I nodded. "He's my friend. I don't want him to get the wrong idea. I want him to understand that it's not a big deal."

"That's the right thing to do," Katie agreed, nodding.

Randy hopped back on her skateboard and rolled a little ahead. "So, when are you going to do it?" she called over her shoulder.

I paused, thinking. I knew the longer I waited, the harder it was going to be. "Right now," I said firmly.

"Wow. Do you want any of us to go with you?" Randy asked.

I would have loved for all of them to come with me. This was not going to be easy — at all. But I knew I had to do it by myself. "No, that's okay," I replied. I stopped and turned around, explaining, "He lives back this way. I'd better get going, before I chicken out."

"Good luck, Al," Katie said, patting my shoulder.

"Call us later, okay?" said Sabs.

"Definitely," I agreed. "As soon as I get home, okay?"

"All right," Sabs replied. "Good luck, Al!"

"Bye!" Katie called out.

"Ciao!" Randy added.

And then they were gone. I walked slowly, trying to figure out what I was going to say to Billy. Before I knew it, though, I was standing in front of Billy's house on Callahan Drive and I still hadn't thought of anything that sounded right to me.

I considered walking around the block a few times to give myself some more time to think of what to say, but then I figured Billy might be looking out the window or something. It would be better to just go in and get it over with.

Squaring my shoulders, I went up to the front door and rang the bell. A moment later, Billy opened the inside door.

"Hi, Billy," I said, trying to smile at him. I searched his face, trying to figure out what kind of mood he was in, but it was hard to tell through the screen door.

"Allison?" Billy asked, sounding surprised. "What are you doing here?"

Taking a deep breath, I said, "I have to talk to you." I could hear my voice wavering, and that made me even more nervous.

"Well, come on in," Billy said. He opened the screen door and held it open for me as I stepped inside.

There was a kind of intense look in his blue-gray eyes, but all he said as he led the way into the living room was, "What's up? Can I get you something to drink?"

I shook my head, wishing that Arizonna had never asked me out, that I had never said yes, that this was all over with — that the whole thing had never happened.

"Billy . . ." I began and then paused, looking down at my hands. I took another deep breath and let it out, then said, "Arizonna asked me out, and I said yes."

Looking up, I watched Billy's eyes turn grayer and more distant. "Well, what do you want, a medal?" he asked in this sarcastic voice.

"Billy —"

"Why did you come here, Allison?" he interrupted angrily. "What are you looking for? You want to see if I'm jealous or something?"

"Billy — " I tried again, but he just kept yelling at me.

"I'd have to care to be jealous, Allison. But I don't care!"

With that, Billy stuffed his hands in his jeans pockets and stormed out of the house, leaving me there in his living room. I winced as I heard the screen door slam shut behind him. I felt as if Billy had just slapped my face.

Suddenly, I was angry. I knew Billy was hurt, but he hadn't even given me a chance to explain. That wasn't fair. I jumped to my feet and raced out of the house. "Billy!" I called, catching sight of him stalking down the sidewalk. "Wait up!"

He didn't turn around or slow down at all. I wasn't going to give up, though. This time, I had to make him listen to me. Running as fast as I could, I finally managed to catch up to him a block down Callahan.

Billy must have heard my footsteps, because suddenly he stopped and whirled around to face me. "What do you want, Allison?" he asked in this really cold voice.

"I . . . I have to . . . explain," I began, trying to catch my breath.

He crossed his arms over his chest. "What's to explain?" he asked in that same icy tone. "I already told you I don't care, so why don't you just leave me alone. Better yet, why don't you just go find your new boyfriend!"

Then he started walking away from me again, leaving me there feeling frustrated and angry.

All of the sudden, I exploded. "I have to explain," I shouted at him, planting my hands on my hips. "And you're going to listen to me. Then you can do whatever you want, all right?"

That sure made Billy stop and look at me. I think he was probably a little shocked at hearing me yell. I was pretty shocked myself. I hardly ever raise my voice.

"What I was going to say to you, before you rushed out of the house," I continued in a softer voice, "was that I told Arizonna I'd go out with him because I didn't want to hurt his feelings. I like him a lot."

I could see Billy's jaw clench, and that awful dark expression came into his face again.

"As a friend," I added quickly. "I'm really glad I met him, but I never expected that he was going to ask me out. And I didn't know what to say, so I just said yes. It's not like I really want to go out on a date with him."

Billy gave me a skeptical look. "Why not?" he asked.

"Because of you," I said automatically, looking down at my feet.

Suddenly I felt really embarrassed. Billy would never understand why I had agreed to go out with Arizonna. So now I had lost Billy as my friend, and I was standing there making a complete fool of myself. I felt as if I were about to cry.

I couldn't stand there in front of Billy a second longer. It was too humiliating. Spinning around, I walked away as quickly as I could, tears beginning to run down my cheeks.

"Allison!" I heard Billy calling after me, but I didn't slow down. I didn't want to feel any worse than I already did.

"Allison, wait up!" Billy called again. Before I knew it, he had fallen into step next to me.

I glanced at him, brushing the tears from my cheeks with the back of my hand.

"So, did you figure out what you were going to do about the food for Earth Alert yet?" Billy asked.

"What?" I asked, stopping and staring at

him. Now I felt really confused. Of all the things I had expected him to say, that was probably at the bottom of the list.

"Did you guys figure out how you're going to feed all of us hungry seventh graders at Earth Alert?" Billy repeated, giving me a lop-sided smile. For the first time in over a week, he was talking to me in his normal tone of voice.

"Not really . . . Billy . . ." I began, and then stopped. I didn't know what to say.

"Don't sweat it, Allison." He gave me this really serious look, then looked away. Scuffing his sneaker against the sidewalk, he said quiet-ly, "I understand about Arizonna. Sorry I've been a jerk." Then he pulled on the end of my braid. "So about the food for Earth Alert . . ."

I just stared at him, feeling relieved and dazed all at the same time. "Billy, are you try-ing to tell me that you've changed your mind about helping us?"

"Sure," he answered, smiling at me. "I was thinking, the best way to get good food for the whole grade out of $200 is to just make it our-selves."

I looked at him dubiously. "Do you think

we can? That's an awful lot of food."

"But if we all chip in, I'll bet we can do it," he said. "I can help with the shopping and cooking and stuff. The important thing is to plan what we think kids would like to eat and then find food that comes from the Earth, know what I mean?"

As I thought about it, it started to make total sense. "Maybe you're right," I told him after a pause. "I'll call Randy tonight. She's in charge of the food committee."

Grabbing my hand, Billy smiled at me and said, "Let's go see what your mother's making for dinner. I hope it's fried chicken. Maybe I can get an invite out of her."

I laughed again and squeezed Billy's hand. My mother had gotten used to Billy showing up at dinnertime. He wouldn't have to do much persuading to get a dinner invitation out of her.

We didn't say anything as we walked, and it felt nice to have our old, friendly silence back. I couldn't help wondering about Arizonna, though. I knew I was going to have to tell him the truth — that I didn't really want to go out on a date with him, unless it was just as friends.

But I had no idea of how I was going to say that without hurting him. Sometimes life really seems complicated. And this was definitely one of those times.

Chapter Six

Allison calls Randy that night:

RANDY:	*Buona sera.*
ALLISON:	Randy?
RANDY:	How ya' doing, Al? How'd it go?
ALLISON:	Hi, Randy. It went fine. I told Billy, and then he came over for dinner. In fact, he just left.
RANDY:	You told Billy that you're going to the movies with Arizonna, and then he came over for dinner? You can't be serious.
ALLISON:	(Giggling) I guess he was a little mad at first.
RANDY:	Only a little? Come on, out with it, Al.
ALLISON:	Well . . . he stormed out of his house when I told him and left me sitting in his living room. But I ran after him —

RANDY: You ran after him? I don't believe it! Don't tell me you were mad.

ALLISON: A little. After I caught up to Billy, I told him what had happened and that I didn't really want to go out with Arizonna, but that I didn't know how to say no without hurting him.

RANDY: That was it?

ALLISON: I guess so. After I explained everything to Billy, he said he understood about Arizonna and apologized for being mean. And then he just asked me about the food for Earth Alert.

RANDY: (Groaning) Don't remind me. We still have to figure something out.

ALLISON: Not anymore. Billy had a great idea. He thinks we should make everything ourselves.

RANDY: Hey, great idea! I bet I can talk M into using our kitchen. We have Friday afternoon off to get stuff set up on the field, so we'll have the whole evening to cook. I'll talk to Sabs and Katie about it.

ALLISON: Listen, I'd better go. My English
             paper is waiting.

RANDY: That's not due for two weeks! I
             know, I know. You like to get
             things done ahead of time.

ALLISON: I'll talk to you tomorrow, okay?

RANDY: Cool. I'm glad you and Billy are
             friends again.

(There is a short pause.)

             So, now what are you going to do
             about Arizonna?

ALLISON: I don't know. I don't think it
             would be right to go out with
             him, though, if I like Billy. It's not
             really fair. I think I have to tell
             Arizonna the truth.

RANDY: When are you going to do it?

ALLISON: (Sighing) As soon as possible.

RANDY: Well, good luck.

ALLISON: Thanks, Randy. Good-bye.

RANDY: *Ciao.*

Randy calls Sabs:

SAM: What's up?

RANDY: Samuel! Randy here. Is Sabrina
             around?

SAM: Hi, Randy. Hold on.

(pause)

SABRINA: Ran? Did you talk to Allison?
              How'd it go? Was Billy really
              mad? What happened? Is Allison
              all right?

RANDY: Breathe, Sabs. You asked me all of
              those questions without taking a
              single breath.

SABRINA: Okay, I'm breathing. So tell me
              what happened!

RANDY: Okay, okay. Al told Billy about
              Arizonna and then he went over
              to her house for dinner. In fact, he
              just left.

SABRINA: That's it? That's all that hap-
              pened?

RANDY: Well, I guess Billy got a little
              ticked and left his house. Allison
              ran after him and told him he had
              to listen to her explanation. So he
              did.

SABRINA: She ran after him? Wow.

RANDY: Yup. She said she was mad.

SABRINA: Al, mad? Unbelievable!

RANDY   I guess it didn't last long, though.

	Hey, by the way, Billy came up with this great idea for the food. We can make it ourselves.
SABRINA:	Hey! Why didn't we think of that? That's a great idea!
RANDY:	Isn't it? I already talked to M. She said we can cook here, and she'll take Katie and Billy and me shopping Wednesday after school.
SABRINA:	Does that mean Billy's helping with the fair again?
RANDY:	You bet. Everything's totally cool with him and Al. Now she's just worried about telling Arizonna.
SABRINA:	Telling him what? Oh, that she likes Billy and doesn't want to go out with him.
RANDY:	In a nutshell. She wants to get it over with, but she doesn't want to hurt him, you know?
SABRINA:	That's going to be tough. I wonder if —
RANDY:	I hate to cut you off, Sabs. But M needs to make some long-distance call to an art gallery in Texas. Can I talk to you later?

SABRINA: Sure. Bye, Randy.
RANDY: *Ciao.*

Sabrina calls Katie:
EMILY: Campbell residence, Emily speak-
             ing.
SABRINA: Hi, Emily. It's Sabs. Is Katie there?
EMILY: Hello, Sabrina. Hold the line for a
             moment, please. I'll get her.
(pause.)
KATIE: Sabs? What's up? Did you talk to
             Allison?
SABRINA: Why was Emily talking like that
             on the phone?
KATIE: (Groaning) It's her mature stage.
             At least that's what my mom
             says. Emily calls me Katherine
             now. I hope it passes soon, what-
             ever it is. I don't know how much
             more I can take.
SABRINA: I know what you mean, and I
             only talked to her for a few sec-
             onds. Listen, Al told Billy, and
             everything's cool. But now she's
             worried that Arizonna's going to
             be really upset when she tells him

	that she can't go out with him.
KATIE:	So, what's she going to do?
SABRINA:	I don't know. Randy had to get off the phone and I haven't talked to Al yet.
KATIE:	You know, it's a shame that Arizonna doesn't know a lot of other girls at Bradley. I mean, maybe he's latching on to Al, just a little, because he's new here.
SABRINA:	I never thought of that.
KATIE:	Sabs, I've got it!
SABRINA:	What? What!
KATIE:	What if Arizonna was the one who broke off the date with Al, instead of the other way around?
SABRINA:	How are we going to get him to do that?
KATIE:	Well, what if he liked someone else?
SABRINA:	Yeah, but who?
KATIE:	Well . . . you like Arizonna, don't you?
SABRINA:	(Shocked) Katie! (She giggles.) I guess I do like him.
KATIE:	And you don't want him to get

hurt, right? Maybe if you just got to know him a little better . . .

SABRINA: He would be the one to decide a date with Al isn't such a great idea! Do you think it would work? I mean, I really would like to get to know Arizonna better. Oh my gosh, I'd better go check my magazines and see if there are any articles on surfing. I'm going to call Al right now and see what she thinks — what if she thinks it's a bad idea?

KATIE: Relax, Sabs. It's a good idea. (She sighs.) I don't suppose Randy said if she thought of anything for the food yet.

SABRINA: Oh — I almost forgot! Billy came up with this idea that we should do the food ourselves. Doesn't that sound like a great idea?

KATIE: Do you think we can make enough?

SABRINA: I'm sure we can. I still can't believe Stacy rented all those rides without talking to us first.

KATIE: That was typical. We shouldn't let
            it bother us.

SABRINA: I'm just glad Arizonna told her
            off.

KATIE: Well, I hope that kids come to our
            part of the fair, too. I mean, those
            games of Al's sound really fun.
            But all I hear kids talking about is
            the roller coaster.

SABRINA: Don't worry about it. Substance
            always wins out over surface.

KATIE: Where'd you read that?

SABRINA: I just made it up. Why?

KATIE: It sounds good. I'm going to write
            it down, okay? I don't want to
            forget it.

SABRINA: Cool. My first memorable quote
            and I'm not even a famous actress
            yet.

Katie laughs.

SABRINA: Well, I better call Allison. It's get-
            ting late.

KATIE: Okay. Good night.

SABRINA: Bye.

Sabrina calls Allison:

ALLISON: Hello? Allison Cloud speaking.

SABRINA: Al, it's Sabs. Listen, I just talked to Randy, and she told me about Billy and Arizonna. I don't know how you're planning to tell Arizonna, but I have an idea.

ALLISON: I don't know how to tell him, but I know I have to. He's going to be hurt, though.

SABRINA: Well, here's my idea. What if you don't tell him?

ALLISON: Sabs! I have to! It's not fair otherwise.

SABRINA: What I mean is, what if Arizonna told you?

(There is a long pause.)

ALLISON: Told me what?

SABRINA: That he didn't want to go on a date with you, that he just wants to be friends.

ALLISON: Why would he tell me that?

SABRINA: He would if he liked another girl. See, Katie and I were talking before, and we figured that if he made friends with someone else,

74

maybe that would take some pressure off of you to be his best friend.

ALLISON: But who? How?

SABRINA: Well . . . me.

ALLISON: What! Sabrina, I think I'm missing something. You better start from the beginning.

SABRINA: Katie's the one who suggested it. Arizonna's cute and everything, and I guess I would like to get to know him better. We figured that if I tried a little harder to make friends with him . . . Oh, I don't know, maybe it's not such a great idea. I mean, what if he doesn't like me?

ALLISON: Sabs, I'm sure he'll really like you once he gets to know you, but I still think I should tell Arizonna myself that I don't think Saturday's date is a good idea.

SABRINA: But, Al, if my plan works, Arizonna won't get hurt, you won't be upset, and Billy won't be mad at you.

ALLISON: I guess I can't talk you out of it.

SABRINA: Well, all I'm saying is wait a little while and maybe you won't have to tell him. Anyway, I heard about Billy's idea for the food. Olivia's taking us to do the shopping Wednesday after school. So does that mean he's not mad anymore?

ALLISON: I don't think so. He volunteered to help shop and everything.

SABRINA: Good, because we've got a lot to do. Listen, I'd better get going. I read an article last month about surfers in one of my magazines. I've got to find it. I read in *Young Chic* that sharing interests is the key in developing friendships.

ALLISON: Good luck, Sabs. I hope the plan works.

SABRINA: Me too. I'll see you in homeroom on Monday, okay?

ALLISON: Good night, Sabs.

SABRINA: Night, Al.

Chapter Seven

"Have you guys seen Sabs today?" Randy asked, coming over to Katie and me in third-period homeroom on Monday morning.

Katie shook her head. "She was late to first period so I didn't catch her at our locker," she said. "Why? Sabs is here, isn't she?"

"Oh, definitely," Randy commented with a grin. "And you should see her!"

I suddenly got a funny feeling in my stomach. "Does this have anything to do with her plan to get to know Arizonna?" I asked.

"Babes!" Sabs called out just at that moment, as she breezed into homeroom. "What's up?"

She was wearing an oversize, cropped turquoise T-shirt and cutoff denim shorts over white long johns. A pair of sunglasses dangled at the end of a neon orange cord around her neck that matched her orange high-top sneakers. The brim of her bright yellow baseball cap was turned up and she had a white UCLA sweatshirt thrown over her shoulders. The only thing she was missing was a tan.

"What did I tell you?" Randy asked, holding up two fingers and giving Sabs the peace sign.

"School is just, like, *too very* today," Sabs announced as she slipped into her seat. "Dudettes," she added, giggling, "the plan is, like, working already. I just happened to be walking by Arizonna's house and, like, we ended up walking to school together."

Katie raised an eyebrow at Sabs. "You just happened to be there?"

"Wow, Sabs," I said, noticing the I'd Rather Be Surfing button that she'd pinned to her sneaker. "When you decide to share a guy's interests, you really go all the way!" I had to admit she looked impressive.

Sabs giggled again. "I played Beach Boys albums the whole time we were working on our posters yesterday. And I took a bath in salt water this morning to make me feel as if I were in the ocean."

"Aren't you going to a lot of trouble?" I asked. "Maybe I should just tell Arizonna the truth myself."

"Like, not a problem," Sabs replied, putting her sunglasses on. "It's totally gnarly anyway, babe. I think that means I'm having a really good time doing this. All this surfing stuff is fun!"

Just then the bell rang, and Sabs swiveled around in her seat so she faced forward. She pulled her sunglasses off just as Ms. Staats walked into the classroom.

Halfway through English, Stacy and Eva walked into the classroom and told Ms. Staats that they had an important announcement.

"As you all know," Stacy began, flipping her blond hair over her shoulder, "the Earth Alert Fair is only days away."

I sat forward in my chair. Why was Stacy talking about the Earth Alert Fair? We hadn't discussed making any announcement during the meeting we'd had at Eva's house on Saturday.

"Since no one else has done anything about ticket sales . . ." Stacy went on, looking smugly in my direction.

"What are you talking about, Stacy?" Randy asked loudly, cutting Stacy off. "Tickets are being sold on the day of the fair. We all agreed on that, remember?"

"Well, Eva and I decided that it would be better to sell them in advance," Stacy retorted.

"Who died and left you king?" Sabs asked, obviously forgetting her surfer lingo for the moment. "You and Eva can't just decide something without consulting everyone else on the planning committee."

Eva gave Stacy a look that said they obviously didn't care what everyone else wanted. "We've been to five homerooms already and sold a lot of tickets," Eva said smugly. "I think that says a lot about who had the right idea."

"And we'll have more tickets for sale in the cafeteria at lunch," Stacy continued.

I knew I should be speaking up along with my friends, but I felt weird about having a big fight right in the middle of English. Ms. Staats had cleared her throat a few times, I'd noticed, but everyone was too caught up in the argument to pay any attention.

"If you've sold some already, you can just hand the money over to Al," Randy was saying. "She's the chairperson."

Stacy gave me a dismissive sort of look

before saying, "Co-chairperson. And I'm the other one, so I guess I can be in charge of the money if I want to. I might as well be, anyway, since this money happens to be helping to pay the balance on the roller coaster and the rest of the stuff we rented."

"You can't do that!" Sabs exclaimed, jumping out of her seat.

"Girls!" Ms. Staats said loudly and firmly, stepping forward. "That's quite enough." She looked slowly from Stacy and Eva, to Randy, Sabs, Katie, and me. "I think it's admirable that you're all concerned about saving our environment, but you'll have to learn to live peacefully together on the planet, too. This is obviously a problem you'll have to work out among yourselves."

She gently ushered Stacy and Eva to the door, saying, "I'd suggest that you all get together and agree on one plan before you disrupt any more classes."

I hardly even paid attention to the rest of class, which is very rare for me. But I kept thinking about Stacy keeping all the fair money. With her in charge of it, there probably wouldn't be anything left for our recycling project.

After class, I left ahead of my friends. I wanted to be alone to think for a minute. Being outside in the fresh air always helps clear my mind, so I went to sit outside the school's front door. The rides did have to be paid for, I reminded myself. What did it matter who kept the money before then? And even though Stacy and Eva were acting like jerks, I guessed it didn't matter as along as we sold a lot of tickets. The rest of the preparations were coming along great, and that was what really mattered.

It took only a minute for me to start feeling better. Getting up, I went to my locker to drop off my books. I had just opened it when I heard Arizonna's voice behind me. "Allison Cloud," he said.

I turned to find him grinning at me.

"Hi, Arizonna." I dumped my books inside and grabbed my lunch bag. I knew I wouldn't be able to act like myself around him, when I really didn't think going out with him was a good idea at all. Standing there, I decided that I'd better tell him that I couldn't go.

When I turned back to him, Arizonna was holding up another friendship bracelet. "My best buddy in L.A. sent me this," he said, handing it to me. "I got it yesterday. I want you to have it."

"But you already gave me one," I protested, holding up my left wrist to show him the first one he'd given me. The next thing I knew Arizonna had tied the new bracelet onto my wrist next to the first!

"You can never have too many, " he told me.

Great going, Allison, I thought miserably. How are you going to cancel the date now?

"Um, Arizonna . . ." I said aloud, but I couldn't seem to get any farther than that.

He brushed his hair out of his eyes and looked at me. "I think it's really cool that we're going to hang together for a movie Saturday," he went on.

I opened and closed my mouth a few times before finally giving up. "Well, um, thanks for the bracelet," I said lamely.

I closed my locker, and we started walking toward the cafeteria. I didn't see how I could ever tell him the truth about the date now. If he didn't change his mind on his own, I would just have to go out with him.

"Al, Arizonna!" Randy called out as soon as we walked into the cafeteria. "Back here!" She and Katie were sitting at an empty table near the back of the crowded room.

"Hey, guys," Randy said as we walked over and sat down. "Are you ready to cook?" she asked, pulling her drumsticks out of her back pocket and drumming them against the table-top. "We've got a lot of food to make."

"It'll be a happening thing," Arizonna replied, opening his lunch bag. He pulled a quart of orange juice out and put it on the table in front of him. "You're going to be there, aren't you, Allison Cloud?"

I nodded. "And just about everyone else who's working on the fair, too." Even though I might end up going out with him on Saturday, I didn't want Arizonna to think that making the food was going to be a date, too.

Just then Sabs came up to the table and sat down next to Arizonna.

Arizonna looked up at Sabs and gave her a big smile. "Hey, Sabs. What's up?"

"Are you going to catch the nationals on television this Sunday?" Sabs asked Arizonna while opening her milk and taking a sip.

Randy looked up from stirring her yogurt. "Nationals of what?" she wanted to know.

"The pro surfing championship in Hawaii," Arizonna explained excitedly, brushing his blond bangs off his forehead. "Major deal."

"Definitely," Sabs added with a knowing nod.

Arizonna turned to look at Sabs, and I thought I noticed a kind of fresh interest in his pale eyes. "Like, I never knew you were into surfing, Sabs," he said.

"Totally," Sabs told him.

"You know, a major buddy of mine from L.A. is at the nationals right now," Arizonna said.

"He's ranked number five in the country, or something," Arizonna continued. "He used to tell my other buddies and me to turn pro."

As he and Sabs kept talking, Randy leaned over to Katie and me and whispered, "How does she know so much about surfing all of a sudden?"

"Her magazines," I explained, giggling.

"But you know, she looks as if she's really into it."

"Gnarly," Randy whispered back, grinning.

"How's it going, Allison?" Billy asked, coming up to our table. He handed me an apple, saying, "I already ate one of these. Want this one?"

"Hi, Billy," I replied, taking the apple. "Thanks." It felt really nice to know that things were back to normal between us.

"What's with Sabs?" Billy wanted to know, nodding his head toward the other side of the table.

"She and Arizonna have found a mutual interest," Randy replied, leaning behind me to whisper to Billy.

"Surfing," Katie added, giggling again.

"I didn't know Sabs was into that," Billy commented.

Randy, Katie, and I looked at each other and cracked up.

"Well, she is now," Randy said, getting control of herself.

We spent the rest of the period talking about our menu for Earth Alert. I hoped a lot of people would show up to help — there were tons of kids in the seventh grade to feed. My friends seemed pretty excited about it, though — except Sabs and Arizonna. Well, I knew they were excited about it, too, but they didn't have a lot to add to the rest of our conversation at the moment. They were too busy talking surfing, and catching waves and deep tans to pay much attention to us.

It was beginning to look as if everything might work out after all. So why did I have these little tiny doubts in the back of my mind?

Chapter Eight

For the rest of the week, I was so busy preparing for the fair that I didn't have time to think about Saturday's date with Arizonna.

Every day after school I helped Sabs and Randy in the gym with the mural. The rest of the time, we were putting up the posters Sabs's committee had made and planning the games and entertainment.

Planning the games wasn't too hard. Arizonna and Laurel came over to my house on Tuesday afternoon, and we talked some more about the Native American games I had learned from my parents and grandparents. Then we decided which ones would be the best for the fair. I had been afraid they would think the games were silly, but they seemed really excited about them.

The food for the fair was the thing that took the most preparation. Since Billy had come up with the idea for making our own food, he joined Randy and Katie on the food committee instead of working on the games. They all went shopping with Randy's mother on Wednesday evening. On Friday, we arranged to meet at Randy's by six o'clock — ready to cook.

"Do you think we'll have enough?" Katie asked worriedly on Friday evening as she, Randy, and I lined up all the food supplies on Randy's kitchen table. "This doesn't look like enough to feed the whole seventh grade."

"Don't worry about it, Katie," Randy replied, pulling all of the pots, pans, and mixing bowls out of the cabinets and setting them on the counters.

I grabbed the jars of honey and maple syrup they had bought, putting them on the table with the other things. "I'm starting to feel really nervous," I admitted. "I mean, what if Stacy's right and all the kids just come to ride the roller coaster. Didn't you see them all watching the setup this afternoon at the football field?"

"That's true," Randy admitted. "No one was down in the soccer field with us."

"Don't worry, Al," Katie said. "I mean, we didn't even mention the rides on the posters, just the environment, and everyone I've talked to seems really excited. I'm sure people will be there for all of the fair.

I hoped she was right. "Where's everyone else?" I asked.

Katie and Randy looked at each other and giggled.

"Arizonna had dinner over at the Wellses' tonight," Katie explained.

"Really?" I said. For the first time since the beginning of the week, I remembered about tomorrow's date.

"Yup," Randy said. "He and Sabs have been spending a lot of time together."

I was glad they were getting along, but Arizonna still hadn't said anything to me about canceling the date. The more I thought about it, the less I felt like going out with him.

Sighing, I set up Randy's juicer at one end of the kitchen counter. "I guess I'd better start turning these into juice," I said, pointing to about two dozen packages of fresh carrots that were piled up next to the juicer. I was amazed at the color the juice turned out. I had never realized how orange carrot juice is.

Just as I started on the second bag of carrots, the doorbell rang.

"I've got it!" Randy's mother sang out, appearing from the back of the house.

Olivia's an artist, and she needs a lot of light and space to work. So she bought a barn for her and Randy to live in. It's doesn't have stalls and hay in it or anything, but the inside was converted into a house. Randy's room is this really cool sleeping loft, and Olivia's studio is in the back part of the barn.

"Hey, Olivia," I heard Sam say as Randy's mother opened the door.

"Hi, guys," Olivia replied, letting him, Nick, and Jason into the house.

Nick made a face as he headed toward us in the kitchen. "Are you guys sure we can't just get a hot dog stand or something?"

"Don't even think about it, Nick!" Katie said, shaking one of the Zaks' wooden spoons at him.

Throwing up his hands in surrender, Nick said, "All right! all right!"

"What do you want us to do?" Jason asked.

Randy looked behind the guys toward the empty doorway. "Hey, where are Sabs and Arizonna?"

"Here we are!" Sabs cried a moment later as

she and Arizonna came through the door. She ran over to us. "Did we miss anything?"

I shook my head. Sabs is the kind of person who can't stand to be left out of things. "We're just starting," I assured her.

"Hey, dudes!" Arizonna said as he walked over to the kitchen area and gave Katie, Randy, and me high fives. I noticed that he didn't say anything special to me.

"Okay, so what do you want us to do?" Sabs asked. She was wearing Arizonna's baseball cap and she gave me a thumbs-up sign when Arizonna had his back turned. I grinned back at her. It seemed as if things were working out between them. I was really happy for them, but I still felt funny not telling Arizonna myself how I felt about our date tomorrow.

"Well, we're going to have all these fruit and vegetable drinks instead of soda," Katie explained, answering Sabs's question. "Why don't you and Arizonna start peeling the bananas and squeezing oranges and lemons?"

"Okay, team, let's roll!" Randy added. She pressed the play button on the tape recorder that sat on the floor by the kitchen wall and started drumming her fingers on the table as the song started. Then she picked up a hammer from the counter and handed it to Nick.

"What's this for?" he asked, staring at it.

Katie handed Sam a can of shelled walnuts and a plastic bag. "You guys have to crush all of these nuts for the brownies," she explained.

"With a hammer?" Nick asked.

"Right," Randy replied. "Put the nuts in a plastic bag and pound away. They should be pretty crushed, but not too fine."

Jason shot a dubious look at Sam. "Very specific," Jason joked.

"Well, Mr. McKee," Katie said, giving him a recipe card, "you can be in charge of the brownies. Here's the recipe, and here's a mixing bowl. The ingredients, as you can see, are everywhere."

"There's no sugar in this!" Jason exclaimed, after studying the recipe for a moment.

"That's because these brownies are sweetened with fruit juice, maple syrup, and honey," I answered. "And they're made with whole wheat flour. All-natural brownies. You know, to fit into Earth Alert."

"I don't know, Al," Sam said, between hammer bangs. "It doesn't sound great."

"Sam, you've eaten these before," Sabs pointed out. "The last time I had a sleepover at our house, Randy brought these brownies."

Sam contorted his face into this really exaggerated look of horror. "We ate natural food brownies?" he asked. "I can't believe I lived through it!"

Sabs rolled her eyes, and I explained, "They don't really taste all that different from regular brownies — they're just thicker or something."

The boys still looked dubious, but they went right to work. With a satisfied nod, Randy turned to Katie and said, "We'd better get to work on these pita bread pizzas. Do you want to grate the cheese?"

Three and a half hours later, the brownies were all cooked, cut up, wrapped, and in boxes; the four juice dispensers from Fitzie's were filled with carrot juice, lemonade, tomato and celery juice, and orange juice. Twelve pounds of mozzarella cheese were grated, and Randy's pizza sauce was simmering on the stove. Nick and Jason were washing dishes, while Arizonna, Sabs, and Katie chopped fruit for the fruit salads that we were going to put into hollowed-out watermelon shells.

Sam and I were making pretzel dough, but I was pretty quiet while we worked. I couldn't help thinking that one thing was still missing: Billy.

I had been sure he would help us with the cooking, but he hadn't shown up yet, or even called. Maybe I had been wrong to assume that he understood about my date with Arizonna. After all, Billy had changed from the games committee to the food. Maybe the fact that Arizonna was working with me on the games had something to do with that. And to make matters worse, it was beginning to look as if I were going to have to go on the date, since Arizonna hadn't said anything about not going.

The doorbell rang, breaking into my thoughts. Seeing that I was nearest the door, I called out, "I've got it," and hurried over to answer it. As I opened the door I tried not to get any of the flour from my hands on the doorknob.

Billy was standing on the doorstep, his hands jammed into his jeans pockets. "Hi, Allison," he said.

"Where were you, Billy?" I asked him softly.

"I thought you were going to help us."

For a moment he just looked down at the ground. "I wasn't going to come over tonight, because I know Arizonna's here. But — "

"I'm glad you're here," I said, smiling at him.

"You are? But . . . " Billy began and then let his voice trail off. "You know, you've got flour all over your face." He smiled and brushed it off my cheek with one hand.

"Who's there?" Sabs called from inside.

"We better get to work," I said, looking over my shoulder. "There's still a lot left to do."

"Are you sure?" Billy asked, hesitating on the step. "I don't want to make it hard on you, Allison."

I was so happy he had decided to come, all I could do for a minute was grin. I promised myself never, ever again to get myself in trouble by not being totally honest. As soon as we were finished with the food, I was going to tell Arizonna I couldn't go with him on the date.

"I'm really glad you're here," I told Billy again after a long pause. Grabbing his hand, I pulled him into the kitchen.

"B.D.!" Nick exclaimed, snapping his dish

towel at Billy.

"Great," Sam said, handing Billy some pretzel dough. "You're just in time to tie pretzel knots."

Forty-five minutes later, we had finished. Arizonna and I were washing the rest of the dishes and everyone else was trying to find boxes and bags to put all the food in.

"Listen, Allison Cloud," Arizonna began, at the exact same time as I said, "Arizonna, I want to — "

We both laughed, then Arizonna said, "I was, like, wondering if . . . Man, this is just too very."

"What?" I asked softly.

"I mean, we'll be buddies forever," Arizonna continued, brushing his bangs back. "But, like, I can see that B.D. is, like, your special pal."

I smiled at him, grateful that he'd said that. I guessed that maybe I did have something special with Billy.

Arizonna handed me a bowl he had just washed, and I started to dry it. "And I don't think it would be cool for us to, like, catch a flick when I'm hanging with Sabs," he added.

A wave of relief hit me, and suddenly I realized that everything would be fine — with Billy, and with Arizonna and Sabs and the Earth Alert Fair.

"I'm glad you feel that way," I told Arizonna. "I was feeling kind of funny about the date, too."

"Really?" Arizonna asked. When I nodded, he said, "Allison Cloud, you'll always be my first and best Minnesota buddy."

Then he leaned over and whispered, "Listen, don't tell Sabs, but I know that she doesn't know, like, the first thing about surfing."

I couldn't help it. I burst out laughing. "What's so funny?" Sabs asked, coming up behind us.

"Nothing," I replied as Arizonna and I grinned at each other. "I'm just happy."

"I know what you mean. I can't wait for tomorrow," Sabs added. "Earth Alert's going to be great!"

Chapter Nine

"These hats are great, Al!" Sabs said, pointing to the green EARTH ALERT baseball cap that topped her curly auburn hair. "It was really nice of your mom to get these for us."

When I got home from Randy's the night before, I had found a box of the caps waiting for me on the kitchen table. My mother had bought enough for everyone on the planning committee. She'd left a note with them, saying how proud she was of us for taking an active role in trying to save our planet.

That had made me feel great, but now I was getting nervous all over again.

"Where is everybody?" Katie asked, reading my thoughts. Her blue eyes were nervously scanning the soccer field, where everything had been set up for today's fair.

I gave a discouraged look toward the mural we had done. It looked really great, but there

were only about ten kids gathered there looking at the painted toucans and spider monkeys
of the mural's rain forest. Otherwise the field
was pretty much empty, except for Katie, Sabs,
Arizonna, Randy, Billy, and me.

"Earth Alert's been open for over an hour,"
I said, sighing, "but hardly anyone's here." I sat
on the edge of the small wooden platform
where Iron Wombat would play later, and rest-
ed my chin in my hands. "I can't believe it. The
only people down here are the ones who
already know how important it is to clean up
the environment."

"Everyone else is up at the football field,"
Sam explained as he, Nick, and Jason came walking over to us.

"That roller coaster's totally bogus, though,"
Nick added.

"What?" asked Sabs, going over to the guys
and standing with her hands on her hips. "You
went on it? How could you!"

Sam, Nick, and Jason all glanced nervously
at each other. "Well . . . we, uh, had to scope out
the competition," Jason stammered.

"It was stupid, though," Sam added quickly.
"Mega Death in Minneapolis is much better.

Stacy's roller coaster doesn't even have a loop or a spiral or anything."

Katie came over to the platform and sat down next to me. "Well, then why is everybody still up there?" she asked.

I was wondering the same thing. I knew that the rides would be the main attraction today, but I had hoped that at least some kids would make it down to the soccer field for the rest of the fair. I looked around at the big awnings we had borrowed from the school. We had set one up on the side of the field for the games, and another one to cover the food and drinks. Even though the field was empty, I thought it looked really inviting.

"Don't worry about it, Allison," Billy told me, grinning. "This is where the food is." He was leaning against one of the hot counters we had borrowed from the cafeteria. It was filled with all the food we had made, and I had to admit it smelled great. I turned to Randy, who was sitting behind her drums on the platform. "Maybe if you guys start playing, that will get everyone's attention," I suggested.

"No problem!" Randy exclaimed, twirling her drumsticks. "We're all set up, and Iron

Wombat's ready to kick — without any energy-eating amplifiers, that is. People will be down soon enough." She pointed a drumstick at the band. "Are you ready?"

A few minutes later, the band was ready, so I left the stage and went over to the juice stand, where Sabs and I were going to be working. As soon as Iron Wombat started to play, all of us started tapping our feet to the beat. I recognized the song they were doing. It was the one Randy and Troy, Iron Wombat's lead singer, had written together for their performance in Battle of the Bands. It was a really beautiful song.

"Hey, can we start playing Hacky Sack?" Jason asked, grabbing one of the little leather balls used to play the game.

"Good idea," I replied. Maybe more kids would come if they saw that we weren't just standing around. Besides, I figured it would be a good way to keep Sam, Nick, Jason, and Billy occupied.

As the guys started kicking the ball to each other, Sabs and I pulled a stack of paper cups out of a box and began putting them on the counter.

"I hope we have enough cups," Sabs commented, eyeing the stack dubiously. "My brother said that a lot of eighth and ninth graders are planning on stopping by."

Glancing at the almost deserted soccer field again, I pointed out, "Sabs, we haven't even sold one cup of juice yet. I'm sure we'll have enough cups."

Three hours later, Sabs almost made me eat my words. We ran out of cups — and juice!

After Iron Wombat began playing, kids started trickling down onto the soccer field. Before I knew it, there were over fifty kids playing Hacky Sack.

Then Sam wanted to start a new game. So I explained "Ghost" to everyone. One person is the "ghost." Everyone else is "living," and they lie face down on the ground in two rows. Each player holds the arms or hands of the person across from him or her. The "ghost" then has to grab the ankles of one of the living people and pull him or her from his or her partner. When the living person finally lets go, he becomes a "ghost helper," and his old partner has to grab on to some other living people quickly before he or she is pulled into the afterlife. The last pair of living people left are the winners.

I didn't know if anyone was going to like this game. I was afraid they might think it was silly. But to my surprise, everyone loved it! They played over ten times. At one point, I noticed that even B.Z. and Laurel were playing. Stacy was probably furious that two of her best friends had left the rides, but it made me feel good about the rest of the fair.

Then it seemed as if everyone descended on the food booths at the same time. I don't think Sabs and I even got a chance to look up for two hours, we were so busy pouring juice.

Iron Wombat and Arizonna had been playing the whole time. They finished by playing the new song Randy and Troy had written about the environment. I could tell by the thoughtful way everyone listened to the song that our Earth Alert message was really getting across.

A bunch of kids started clapping and cheering as the band left the stage, and a few people shouted, "Save our planet!" Then everyone was clapping and shouting together. "Save our planet! Save our planet!"

I was so excited. "Sabs, people are really listening. Isn't it great?"

Sabs's head bobbed up and down excitedly.

"Al, we did it! Everyone came! Wasn't Arizonna terrific!" she said in a rush, leaning toward me so I could hear her over the crowd. "I can't believe he actually dedicated a song to me!" She was doing what she calls her body blush, where she turns red from head to toe.

"He's a really good singer," I told her. Arizonna had played a couple of songs he had written himself, and I thought they sounded better than some of the things I've heard on the radio.

"This is wild!" Randy exclaimed, stopping in front of our booth. "Can I have a glass of juice?"

"We're all out!" Sabs said excitedly, pointing to the four empty dispensers. "I had no idea so many people would drink carrot juice."

"Hey, I think you better straighten your hat, Al," Randy advised.

"Why? Is something wrong with it?" I asked, taking off my baseball cap and smoothing back the strands of hair that had escaped from my braid.

"Because . . ." Randy began, and then paused as the shouts of "Save our planet" died down.

I looked up and saw that Troy Tanner was holding up his hands for quiet.

"And now, I'd like to ask the person responsible for Earth Alert to come up and say a few words . . ." Troy said loudly after the applause had died down.

My whole body went into shock. I don't think anything makes me more nervous than being in the spotlight. "Randy, you didn't," I whispered.

"I did," she replied, grinning at me. "Hey, Al, somebody's got to educate these kids. Go get them to save the planet!"

" . . . Allison Cloud!" Troy finished, waving his hand toward me.

"But — " I began, feeling totally self-conscious. I couldn't get up there in front of the whole grade. What would I say?

I blinked, realizing that over a hundred kids were staring at me. I had no choice. Straightening my shoulders, I put my head up and started walking toward the stage.

"Go get 'em, Allison!" I heard Billy yell. I turned around and saw him sitting on the counter of one of the food booths. He grinned and gave me a thumbs-up sign.

Once on the small stage, I looked out at the large crowd a little nervously.

"Hello, everybody," I said, kind of softly.

"Thank you all for coming to Earth Alert. You all know that our planet is in trouble. There's global warming and nuclear waste. Dolphins and whales are being used as bait to catch tuna fish. We have oil spills and acid rain and endangered species."

As I spoke I started to forget my nervousness. I guess my feelings about saving our environment sort of took over. "The rain forests are being destroyed at the rate of fifty acres every minute!" I said in a louder voice. "This planet is our only home, and we've got to do something before it's too late. If we allow the Earth to be destroyed, where will we go? It's up to us to make a difference. And we can! You all proved that by showing up at Earth Alert and by voting to donate the profits to start a recycling program here at Bradley Junior High! The earth is in trouble, but we can save it! We here at Bradley can make a difference!"

I stopped. There was a long silence, and I wondered if I should say anything else. Then, suddenly, the whole soccer field erupted in cheers. Even if I could have thought of something to add, no one would ever have been able to hear it. So I waved to the crowd, smiled, and stepped off the stage.

Arizonna was at the front of the crowd. When I got off the stage, he came over to me and said, "That was major, Allison Cloud. I'm glad you're my friend."

"Me too," I replied, smiling at him. And I was. Arizonna was a special person, and I was really happy he had moved to Acorn Falls.

"You were great!" Katie exclaimed as she, Sabs, and Randy ran over and hugged me.

"Seriously!" Sabs agreed. "You know, you should go into politics. I had no idea you could make a terrific speech like that."

"That was wild!" Randy added. "You really helped everyone to feel that we can do something!"

"Earth Alert's a definite success, Al!" Sabs exclaimed. "And it was all because of you!"

"I couldn't have done it without you guys," I replied, feeling really lucky that they were my friends.

Just then, someone tugged on my braid, and I turned around to see Billy.

"I was nervous for you," he told me. "But you didn't need it, Allison. You were fantastic!" Then he leaned over and squeezed my hand.

Chapter Ten

"Where did all this garbage come from?" Sabs asked later that afternoon, holding the biodegradable garbage bag open for me as I dumped a bunch of paper cups into it.

"I'm amazed at this mess," Randy agreed, dropping more paper plates and cups into the bag Katie held. "And you guys should see the football field where the rides were. It's even worse!"

I nodded. I'd seen the football field earlier, and I was feeling pretty discouraged. We had gone to all this work to make the kids at Bradley environmentally aware, and here the four of us were picking up tons of garbage that no one had bothered to throw in the garbage cans we had put in convenient spots all over the place.

"Where's Stacy?" Katie wanted to know. "I mean, the rides were her part of the fair, weren't they? Isn't it her responsibility to get the football field cleaned up?"

I nodded. "But if she's gone home, we're the ones who will have to make sure there's no litter left there," I pointed out. "At least, I will. I mean, I was in charge of Earth Alert."

"Hey, we'll help, Al," Randy put in. "We wouldn't leave you to do this alone."

Sabs turned to look at Sam, Jason, and Nick, who were just arriving. "And I'm sure you guys will be happy to help, too, won't you?" she said in a voice that told them they really didn't have much choice.

"Happy to do what?" Jason asked suspiciously.

I tugged on the brim of my EARTH ALERT cap and told them, "We've got to clean the football field, too."

Just then, Billy rounded the corner by Randy's rain forest mural. He was holding four long wooden sticks with sharp metal points at the end. "Look what Mr. McManus gave me. He was cleaning the front windows of the school when I walked past."

"Cool!" Sam exclaimed. He, Nick, and Jason grabbed three of the four sticks and the four boys headed up to the football field.

"Hey, Sabs," Randy said suddenly. "What do you have on your wrist?"

Sabs held up her right arm, which had about ten friendship bracelets tied around it. "Oh, you mean these?" she asked. "Arizonna gave them to me this afternoon when the fair ended."

"Ooohh!" Katie teased. "This must be getting serious. Allison got only got two bracelets."

Sabs turned bright red and shrugged her shoulders.

Suddenly I caught sight of about ten guys walking across the field toward us. "I wonder who they are?"

"Yo!" Randy exclaimed, following my gaze. "Here come the troops!"

"It's the guys on the hockey team," Katie said. "All right! I saw Scottie and Flip this afternoon and they offered to round up the hockey team to help us clean up. Cool."

After that, we cleaned up in no time. A half-hour later, the soccer field was spotless, and we all headed up to the football field to see if the other guys were finished.

"I don't believe these guys!" Sabs exclaimed

when we saw them.

Sam, Jason, and Nick were throwing their sticks around as if they were javelins. Arizonna and Billy were pretending to fence each other with their sticks. I couldn't help laughing, but I noticed that only about half the field was picked up.

"Let's get to work, guys," I said, as we got closer.

Twenty minutes later we had all the grounds cleaned up, and we headed to Fitzie's. The idea was to celebrate about the Earth Alert Fair being such a big success, but I still felt a little depressed. I didn't want to say anything to ruin everyone else's good mood, but I should have known my friends would notice.

"What's up, Al?" Randy asked. "Are you mad that Stacy went home?"

Sabs laughed. "I never expected her to stay," she said. "Cleaning up is hard work. Stacy the Great wouldn't have risked a broken nail to help us out."

"Not a problem," Arizonna said, reaching over for some of Sabs's french fries. "We got it all, like, under control without her."

"So, then what's wrong?" Randy asked me,

getting back to her original question.

"I'm just a little depressed about Earth Alert," I admitted, stirring my soda with the straw.

Katie shot me a concerned look over her vanilla sundae. "What's wrong?" she asked.

"Well," I answered slowly, "we just had an Earth Alert Fair to make everyone more environmentally aware, and people still littered."

"But . . . we made everyone a little more aware of the problem. That's a start, isn't it?"

I just nodded. I knew they were trying to make me feel better, but I still felt disappointed that we hadn't been able to make a bigger difference.

"But you want more than that, right, Allison?" Billy asked, nudging me. "You want to see some real changes. Is that it?"

I sat straight up in the booth and I looked at him. I don't know why I was surprised that Billy knows me that well. "I guess that is it," I told him.

"Well, what do you want to do?" Randy asked, slurping up the rest of her chocolate milk shake.

"Think globally, act locally," Arizonna

announced. "That's the answer, Allison Cloud."

"What?" I asked. But as I thought it over, I realized he was right. I shouldn't feel discouraged. I got everyone thinking about the large global issues and saving the planet. Now, I had to show them what they could do to make a difference right here in Acorn Falls.

Suddenly, I knew just what to do.

"Here's your sign, Al," Randy said, handing me a picket sign.

It was Monday morning, and Randy, Katie, and I were standing on the front steps of Bradley holding picket signs. One side of our signs said things like "Save the Planet" and other global statements. The other side said, "Ban Styrofoam From Bradley."

We had decided that we had to act locally, and what better place to start than at our school. The cafeteria uses styrofoam trays and cups. I thought cardboard trays made out of recycled paper would be much more environmentally conscious.

"Hi, guys," Sabs said, practically running

up to us. "Sorry I'm late."

"No problem," Randy replied, handing her a sign.

As some kids started to arrive Katie held up her sign. "This is really exciting," she said. "I can't believe we're breaking the rules like this."

"It's for a good cause," I reminded her. "I just hope we don't get into too much trouble."

A minute later, Mr. Hansen walked up to the front door where we were all standing.

"What's going on here?" he asked, frowning as he eyed our signs.

"They're picketing," Stacy pointed out, coming up behind her father. She obviously loved the idea of getting us into trouble.

"Well, what's the meaning of this?" Mr. Hansen demanded. "What are you girls picketing?"

Gripping my sign a little more tightly, I faced Mr. Hansen and replied firmly, "We're protesting against the Styrofoam trays that the school uses in the lunchroom."

The disapproving way he was looking at me almost made me want to back down. No one ever said that acting locally was going to be easy, I reminded myself. Change is always a struggle. That was what I had read, and now I could see that it was true, even on a small level.

"Picketing is against school rules," Mr. Hansen said, scowling.

"That's right," Stacy agreed, egging him on.

"But — " Randy began to protest.

"And any act against school rules automatically results in detention," Mr. Hansen cut her off. "I'm sorry, girls. But if you've got something to say, you have to go through the proper channels."

"You mean we should go to school board meetings?" Randy blurted out. "Or maybe we should write a letter to the editor of the school paper?"

I knew what Randy was thinking — that going through those channels would take a long time and might not accomplish anything.

"Exactly," Mr. Hansen replied, his eyes narrowing a little. I could tell that he was getting angry. "I'm sorry, but you four girls have just gotten yourselves detention. I'll see you in my office after school."

For a long moment, no one moved. Even the crowd of kids gathered around us was quiet. I felt awful. I mean, I knew my friends all thought it was worth it to fight for a cleaner environment. But so far, all my big idea was accomplishing was getting all of us in trouble.

I was wondering what to do next, when I heard someone murmuring about getting out of his way. The next thing I knew Billy emerged from the crowd. He jumped up to the step below the one I was standing on and took my sign.

"I guess you'll have to give me detention, too," he told Mr. Hansen, "since I'm picketing."

Mr. Hansen gave Billy a weary look. "If that's the way you want it, Mr. Dixon," the principal said grimly. "I'm sure we can find the room in detention for you as well."

"I hope there's room for me, too," Sam announced, stepping up next to Sabs.

A vein in Mr. Hansen's forehead started bulging. I could tell he was not happy with the way things were working out.

"Me too," Nick said as he and Jason stood up next to Sam.

Arizonna was the next to join us. "Dude, the environment is an important issue," he said, taking my sign from Billy.

I couldn't believe it. Everyone was actually

standing up to Mr. Hansen. Maybe now he would realize that what we were fighting for was an important issue. I decided I had to speak up — for me and my friends and our cause.

"Mr. Hansen," I began, "I guess you're right about going through the proper channels, but what about free speech? Why is picketing against school rules? Even though we're only students, we're still entitled to our First Amendment rights, aren't we? Besides, we feel it's really important that we do something to stop the destruction of our planet. If you asked me, I'd say you should be pretty happy that we care enough to do something about it," I continued, ignoring Stacy. "We really believe in this."

Mr. Hansen opened and shut his mouth a few times. It was the first time I ever saw our principal at a loss for words. I held my breath, waiting to hear what he would say.

After a long pause, Mr. Hansen cleared his throat and said, "I'm sorry, but picketing is still against the school rules. I'll see you all in detention."

There was a loud groan, but Mr. Hansen

held up his hand to quiet us. "But," he added in a softer voice, "maybe we should talk about this Styrofoam tray business. I've never really considered the ramifications before. I'll see what I can do about getting recycled cardboard trays."

I couldn't believe it, but then Mr. Hansen actually smiled. "I applaud your dedication to this cause," he told us. "And I'm very pleased to see that Bradley's doing its job by turning out determined students who care."

Loud cheering rose from everyone in the crowd, but I noticed that Stacy was still glaring at us.

"But you still have detention. And I'll have to ask you to put your signs away now," Mr. Hansen finished. Then he went inside.

"I guess we don't need these anymore," Katie said. She started to put her sign in the trash can, but I grabbed it from her.

"We don't want to give people the message that we're going to throw away our cause now," I said, collecting the signs from everyone. "People should know that the fight to save the environment never stops."

A lot of people cheered, and I could feel

myself turning red as we all followed Mr. Hansen into school.

"Hey, Al," Billy said, coming up next to me, "I knew you could do it. You showed people that the earth's problems don't end just because the fair's over. You made a difference."

"Yeah," said Sabs. "From now on, Bradley Junior High is going to be on constant Earth Alert!"

"We all made a difference," I corrected him, grinning at all my friends. "You guys are the best!"

Look for these titles in the GIRL TALK series

★**1** **WELCOME TO JUNIOR HIGH!** Introducing the Girl Talk characters, Sabrina Wells, Katie Campbell, Randy Zak, and Allison Cloud. When our four heroines meet and have to plan the first junior high dance of the year, the results are hilarious.

★**2** **FACE-OFF!** Katie Campbell is just plain fed up with being "perfect." But when she decides to join the boys' ice hockey team, she gets more than she bargained for.

★**3** **THE NEW YOU** Allison Cloud's world turns upside down when she is chosen to model for *Belle* magazine with Stacy the Great!

★**4** **REBEL, REBEL** Randy Zak is acting even stranger than usual. Could a visit from her cute New York friend have something to do with it?

★**5** **IT'S ALL IN THE STARS** Sabrina gets even when she discovers that someone is playing a practical joke on her — and all her horoscopes are coming true.

★**6** **THE GHOST OF EAGLE MOUNTAIN** The girls go on a weekend ski trip, only to discover that they're sleeping on the very spot where the Ghost of Eagle Mountain wanders!

LOOK FOR THE GIRL TALK SERIES!
IN A STORE NEAR YOU!

TALK BACK!

TELL US WHAT YOU THINK ABOUT GIRL TALK

Name _____

Address _____

City _____ State _____ Zip _____

Birthday Day _____ Mo. _____ Year _____

Telephone Number (___) _____

1) On a scale of 1 (The Pits) to 5 (The Max),
how would you rate Girl Talk?   Circle One:

             1   2   3   4   5

2) What do you like most about Girl Talk?

___Characters___Situations___Telephone Talk

Other _____

3) Who is your favorite character? Circle One:

     Sabrina   Katie   Randy

     Allison   Stacy   Other

4) Who is your least favorite character?

_____

5) What do you want to read about in Girl Talk?

_____

_____

Send completed form to :
Western Publishing Company, Inc.
1220 Mound Avenue Mail Station #85
Racine, Wisconsin 53404